**This new book was p**[rinted for the]
**East Anglia Children'**[s Hospice]
**by Bob Able, the auth**[or.]

Please give it back to a charity shop when you have read it
so that it can be sold again to make more money
for worthwhile causes.

# Bobbie And The Spanish Chap

## A Bobbie Bassington Story

### Bob Able

Copyright © 2022 Bob Able

All rights reserved

The characters and events portrayed in this book are fictitious. Any similarity to real persons, living or dead, is coincidental and not intended by the author.

No part of this book may be reproduced, or stored in a retrieval system, or transmitted in any form or by any means, electronic, mechanical, photocopying, recording, or otherwise, without express written permission of the publisher.

# Bobbie and the Spanish Chap

**Introduction**

We first met Roberta 'Bobbie' Bassington in the novel *'Double Life Insurance'*, but there have been enquiries into what happened next to this delightful, infuriating, vivacious, effervescent, fun-loving explosion. If you read that book you may have wondered where her tip-tilted nose, enormous green eyes and capacity for making things go off bang would turn up next.

Well, now it can be told. But for those who need a reminder, here is a brief look at what happened in the recent past.

Of course this little soupçon is really for those who haven't read the earlier book, so feel free to skip to Chapter One, if you have, or don't need a refresher…

*….. Glancing at his phone as it rang, Geoff was pleased to see that the caller was Roberta 'Bobbie' Bassington.*

*This delightful, if rather high-spirited girl was the*

*daughter of his ex-wife's sister, who lived with her mother in the moth-eaten, but once rather grand, family home in Barton Matravers, Wilts.*

*Geoff had always liked Roberta and fortunately his affection was returned. That was just as well for she was a girl of strong passions who, when roused, was quite likely to start something.*

*With her petite frame, vivid auburn hair, pert upturned nose and large green eyes she was certainly very attractive. But those eyes could also shoot flames for up to ten feet if she was thwarted in any of her little plans or schemes, as several of her short-lived boyfriends had found to their cost.*

*Most of the time, however, Roberta was full of fun and a delightful charming girl. At least that was the general view of most of the cloud of hapless, lovelorn suiters who followed her around.*

*These estimable features, apart perhaps from the flame-shooting eyes, were not in evidence however when Geoff answered the call.*

*'<u>Why</u>, Uncle Geoffrey dear, has your wife inflicted her foul company on the old family home with, it would seem, the intention of making an extended stay?' she said.*

*'Eh?' said Geoff, not abreast.*

*'This loathsome aunt seems to have dug herself into the woodwork and refuses even the strongest entreaties to be gone. Have you been being unkind to her? And*

*what suggestion have you for removing this impossible-to-satisfy human complaints department from the once peaceful old home and rolling sunlit lawns of Matravers Hall?'*

*Roberta had recently graduated from Girton College, Cambridge, and given her manner of speech, Geoff wondered if she had been reading a little more Edwardian literature than was good for her.*

*'I'm sorry, I don't think I ...' he blustered.*

*'You heard, you old blister. Why is your estranged wife here when she has a perfectly good house on the outskirts of a very pleasant bit of suburban commuter belt to infest instead?'*

*'I have no idea,' said Geoff, collecting his wits, 'She made no mention of it to me. Is she being a nuisance?'*

*'I should say so! She is a pest and a pestilence and a porcine, petulant problem.'*

*'Now, Bobbie,' chided Geoff gently, 'Would you say "porcine"? Is that any way to describe a loved relative?'*

*'Well, perhaps that was a bit strong, but she has certainly put on weight since I saw her last, and gulps down her meals with an unbecoming gusto, the like of which I have not encountered before in all my young life. I wouldn't mind that so much as Matravers Hall has always done its guests well and been generous with the grub as you know, but I have been turfed out of the blue room to accommodate her spreading bulk, and she parks her*

beastly Citroen in front of my dear little sports car, making a quiet sneak to the local pub for a little peace and quiet jolly difficult without alerting mother!'

Geoff stifled a chortle as he imagined her pique at these little inconveniences.

'I mean to say, fair enough that mother wheels out the fatted calf for her sister, I suppose, but your erstwhile wife had eaten it all before the more permanent members of the household got a look in. And she is never, ever, satisfied.'

'How do you mean?' asked Geoff, who, as it happened, had a fair idea what she meant.

'My dear adopted uncle-by-marriage, even you cannot have failed to notice her wheedling way of wanting things her own way and involving everyone in getting what she wants.
Why this very morning, just after breakfast, mark you, she had us rearranging the furniture in the sitting area of the blue room suite because the sun glinted in the mirror and caught her eye as she was trying to read her book, stretched out on the sofa like a beached whale!'

'A beached whale?'

'Yes, a big-breakfasted, bloated, bulbous, balloon of a beached whale. I'd just watched her consume three sausages, two fried eggs and most of the remaining bacon, after which she finished all the tea in the pot. And this spectacle, I might add, I was forced to endure after something of a late night at Rosy Brice-Waterman's *twenty-first birthday party.'*

*'My wife went to Rosy Brice-Waterman's twenty first birthday party?' asked Geoff incredulously.*

*'No, but I did, you silly old uncle, and the morning head it left me with is still rather troubling me.'*

*'No wonder you are in a bad mood,' Geoff offered.*

*'I'm incandescent, inconvenienced, and incredibly fed up, and what I want to know is what is to be done about it?!'*

*'Well, I don't know that I ...'*

*'No, I suppose your sphere of influence with the lady in question is somewhat reduced following recent events. How is the sparkling dentist by the way?'*

*'Janet is very well, thank you. I hope you will get to meet her soon. I'm sure you two would get on famously.'*

*'Yes well, perhaps we would, but before I run the eye over your new lady-love we must cope with your recent cast-off. It seems mother and I are left to clear up your mess, and were it not for ties of blood, I'm convinced mother would have bopped her with a chair leg by now.'*

*'Is it really that bad?'*

*'It's worse! Look Uncle Geoffrey, couldn't I come and stay with you for a week or two until she blows over? It is awfully inconvenient being down in the country at the moment and mother won't let me go anywhere while your former wife is on the premises, insisting I have to be*

*around to help all the time.'*

*'I thought you regarded Matravers Hall as an earthly paradise?'*

*'It is, or was until recently ...'*

*'Well then?'*

*'Well, all right, yes. The thing is, Uncle Geoffrey, you know how close we have always been and how much I love your company ...'*

*'Come to the point, Bobbie, what are you really after?' said Geoff a little impatiently.*

*'Why, you old sweetie-pie, you always could read me like a book! It's why I regard you with such respect and deep affection, and always look upon you more as a trusted and much loved friend and mentor than just an uncle by marriage ...'*

*'Bobbie!'*

*'Oh, all right. Look, the thing is some friends from Uni have clubbed together to hire a boat for ten days to potter about on the Thames, and I have been invited to join the consortium to lend a bit of glamour to the proceedings. But I can't go if mother continues to insist on my baby-sitting your blasted ex-wife.'*

*'I thought it would be something like that. Why can't your mother look after her herself?'*

*'Ah, that's where the difficulty arises. You see, mother has*

*a longstanding arrangement to go to some literary retreat thing in Wales and read the unsuspecting inmates chunks of her ghastly books, right when this rather jolly trip on the Thames is due to take place.'*

'I see,' Geoff smiled to himself. *Roberta's plans always had little complications like this and rarely gained her mother's unconditional approval.*

'Of course it wouldn't matter at all if your wretched reject hadn't decided to impose herself on us. If I can't shift her I shan't be able to go, and all my hopes and dreams are rather dependent on going.'

'Oh yes? And does this fellow have a name?'

'Fellow? I don't follow you, Uncle Geoffrey.'

'Yes, you do, you little minx. The fellow you hope to go on the boat trip with.'

'Ah, well. There is, I admit, a certain romantic interest in this little tale. You see Rosy Brice-Waterman's brother is going along as it happens …'

'And it is he who invited you?'

'Gosh, Uncle, you are such a detective! As you so cleverly divined, it was he who invited me! However did you work that out?!'

'And by saying you are staying with Janet and I, you will placate your mother and make her think you are under my doting and ever watchful eye, I take it?'

'Something in that, yes.' Roberta paused for breath, 'But none of that works if we can't winkle your horrible ex out of the family home!'

Geoff sighed.

'Roberta, you can always be relied upon to shake Hell's very foundations with your plans and schemes, but I think involving me in your little deception is rather naughty ...'

'You won't do it?'

'I didn't say ...'

'Oh, Uncle Geoffrey, you always used to call me Bobbie when you loved me. Have you forgotten all the fun we had with me sitting on your knee at the piano as you taught me to play 'chopsticks'; or that time we went to the Ritz for tea to celebrate your retirement; or that day at the races when ...'

'Yes, yes, Bobbie. I know. But you ask a lot of me, and I confess I have no plan to get my wife to leave your house yet ...'

'Not yet, perhaps, but you know how clever you are, dear Uncle Geoffrey ... or should I call you Uncle Geoff now, like Janet does ... I'm so looking forward to meeting her, by the way. And I'm so glad you have found happiness and can be with the one you love, while I, trapped in this crumbling old pile, surrounded, not by my lively and attractive peers, but forced to waste my young life *with unrelenting drudgery at the hands of the older generations of our family ...'*

*'Bobbie, please stop! I'm trying to think ...'*

*'You are? You mean you might help after all? I knew I could rely on you, I can't imagine why I thought for a moment that you wouldn't be the knight in shining armour I have always seen you as, riding fearlessly to my rescue in your shining Jaguar ... the same Jaguar that took us all on those lovely sun-drenched picnics, do you remember ...'*

*'I'll hang up if you don't shut up, Bobbie! Now listen,' said Geoff, 'I might have an idea.'*

*-ooOoo-*

*Granted that who could say where Bobbie's little adventures would lead, and episodes in the past did give him pause for thought, but she was grown up now and was entitled to live her own life.*

*To Geoff, a gentle cruise up and down a portion of the Thames in the company of some university friends seemed harmless enough and he resolved to do what he could to make it possible.*

We join them in conversation on the telephone later that week. Geoff is laying out a plan ...

'But we could possibly use it to your, and my advantage.'

'In what way?'

'Well, you see my wife, egged on by her solicitor, is now coming to the boil in frustration about what she has been told is my unwillingness to start the process of selling the house. The facts of the matter, let me say at this point, are quite the reverse of that. This must go no further, Bobbie, but Janet and I are looking to buy a house together, so of course I need to get my share of the sale of the house to make that happen. I can rely on your discretion on that point, can't I Bobbie? I must insist on it remaining just between us.'

'My lips are sealed, Uncle Geoff, 'and even if they put matchsticks between my little toes I shall never tell.' Bobbie stated.

'Matchsticks between your toes? Whatever are you talking about, Bobbie? Why would anyone put matchsticks between your toes?'

'Well, I've no idea actually. I wondered at first if it was anything to do with painting one's toenails when I heard mother reading aloud something about it from one of her books. But then I realised that the baddies, in mother's book I mean, proposed to light the matches to obtain a confession as to where the hero had hidden the keys of the safe, when the flames burned down and caused him discomfort. A silly idea, I thought, when a swift sock on the breezer would bring faster results and add a satisfactory increase to the amount of blood already being sprayed about in that particular section of mother's novel.'

'Yes, well, as I was saying,' said Geoff shaking his head. 'Supposing I let it be known that I was prepared to allow her to get the estate agents in as long as she undertook to handle showing them around, given that my solicitor has put it out that I find it too painful to visit the place which holds so many upsetting memories for me...'

'And I thought the plots of my mothers books were rotten ...' interjected Bobbie.

'If, as I was saying, I insisted that she based herself at the house to meet the estate agents and handle viewings and so on, I believe she would rush back there like greased lightning and you would be released from your Auntie-sitting responsibilities ...'

'Uncle Geoff, you are a wonder! That is pure genius. If my mother could think up clever things like that to put in her books to enable the lovers to meet, she would have them queuing round the block to buy the beastly things!'

'Lovers queuing round the block?' Geoff chuckled.

'No, punters, customers, book buyers, silly! The lovers only meet on paper, but the readers part with hard cash to read about them. Mad isn't it.'

'If it pays the bills ...'

'Oh, Uncle Geoff, you are so clever! I can't see how this wheeze can fail. You have made your favourite niece-by-marriage a very happy young lady. I'm afraid I must go now and do joyful dances on the lawn before I phone my *friend Brice-Waterman and tell him we are on, and I shall soon be draping myself decorously on the prow, or is it the transom, of his elegant river cruiser in the sunshine! Thank you, Uncle Geoff. You are still my knight in shining Jaguar after all!'*

Right. Now lets see what happened next.

# Chapter 1

'I don't think we have met Rosy, have we?' asked Geoff.

'No, I don't think so. You would know if you had. Outdoorsy, all-for-it type. We were up at Girton together,' said Bobbie. 'She was a bit of a blood for rowing and all that sort of thing. Fearsomely bright, of course. One of those clever girls who got into University early. She was a year below me but graduated at the same time and was always heaps of fun.'

'I see,' said Geoff. 'You have been on holiday with her before, haven't you?'

'What? Oh, the foul, frightful, failed river trip you mean. When her awful oaf of a brother put me off boys of his particularly loathsome type for life.'

'Yes. When you came scuttling back here early, halfway through the planned trip, with all sorts of tales of woe.' Geoff smiled at the memory.

'I do not "scuttle", Uncle Geoffrey. I may have made a retreat at a few more m.p.h. than my usual elegant glide, but you could not accuse me of "scuttling"! And

I was sorely pressed by events, so allowances must be made.' Bobbie pulled a face and continued. 'Let's not forget what I had to endure on that revolting old tub Brice-Waterman had the raw cheek to call a River Cruiser. Take, for example, the shower. I shudder at the recollection!'

'Oh, it can't have been that bad. A bit like camping, I would have thought.'

'Camping? You don't really expect a young girl of my delicacy and fragrant loveliness to want to subject herself to anything resembling camping, do you?'

'No, of course not, Bobbie. If you can't spend an hour in the shower followed by another one messing about in the bathroom every morning, you consider the day wasted,' chuckled Geoff.

'Don't tease, Uncle Geoffrey. A girl has to follow her beauty routine, you know. Otherwise the radiant vision you see before you now would just become another fading rose in a sea of so many. To stand out one has to work at it!'

Bobbie danced a few steps towards the front door where she heard Janet turning the key as she returned from work.

Their effusive greetings forced Geoff to shelve his enquiries into Bobbie's no doubt ambitious plans for a while, as the excited conversation flowed backwards and forwards between his two favourite females.
It was not until after supper that he got the chance to

pick up the threads again and press Bobbie further on the plans for her trip abroad.

Janet was asking about Rosy Brice-Waterman and Geoff saw his chance to join in.

'So,' he said now, 'Your idea is to go to Spain with Rosy and visit your boyfriend there?'

'Orlando,' said Bobbie, looking at him censoriously, 'is not my boyfriend in the fullest sense of the word. Well, not yet at least.'

'Oh. But I thought you said …' began Janet.

'I may have mentioned that we have had a few casual dates …' said Bobbie.

'Including a trip to The Proms, the ballet and Goodwood,' interjected Janet.

'Yes, all of that. But he has not yet qualified for the title of "boyfriend". We are still enjoying each others' company as friends.'

Geoff chuckled, which earned him a gentle slap on the arm from a reddening Bobbie.

'I thought he was nice when he picked you up here,' said Janet.

'In his drop-head Porsche …' added Geoff.

'All right. Yes, I admit I like him.' Bobbie squirmed.

'Who wouldn't?' said Janet. 'He works for his father's

international law firm, where it seems he has his own department, dresses like a designer's model and is as handsome as they come!'

'And you said he was well off and had a sexy Mediterranean accent, too,' added Geoff.

'Oh stop it!' blushed Bobbie. 'I grant you he is quite a catch and I'm not immune to his charms. But he still has some good old-fashioned wooing to do before I am prepared to refer to him as a boyfriend.'

'And this trip you plan with Rosy Brice-Waterman might change that?'

'It might. I regard it as another stepping stone along the way,' said Bobbie. 'We shall be visiting him on his home turf, as it were, and seeing him in his native land.'

'Are you going to meet his mother and father?' asked Janet.

'You make it sound like a formal sort of thing.' Bobbie looked surprised. 'The contingency of meeting any parents is not on our somewhat loose agenda. The plan is to soak up some Spanish sun whilst being taken here and there and, no doubt, spoilt by Orlando. There may even be a chance to meet some of his friends and Rosy might select one as a companion during our stay, perhaps.'

'Making up a foursome in sunny Spain. How romantic!' said Janet dreamily.

'Well, be that as it may,' said Geoff. 'We don't really know very much about this Orlando chap, and going to spend a week in a foreign country with him is not like going on a boat on the Thames just down the road, you know. You can't just scuttle back home from Spain if it doesn't work out, Bobbie.'

'Ten days, actually, and we have covered the issue of "scuttling" before, Uncle Geoff.' Bobbie scowled. 'If, like mother, you are proposing to invoke the Spanish Inquisition on the matter, let me say that Rosy and I are staying in a rather nice tourist hotel which we booked through a proper British Travel Agent, and we will be sharing a room. So you can put any of those sort of ideas right out of your head!'

'You will be sharing a room with Rosy?' asked Geoff.

'That is what I said, Uncle Geoffrey. Although, in these enlightened times, it is not really any business of yours, I can state that Orlando and I are at the stage of holding hands occasionally, and nothing more.'

'Holding hands. How romantic!' said Janet.

'I'm sorry Bobbie. I didn't mean to pry. I merely want to be sure you are going to be safe.'

'That's rather sweet, Geoff. But I'm sure Bobbie knows what she is doing,' smiled Janet.

'It is sweet of you to care, yes, Uncle Geoff, and since my father died you have always stepped up to fill the parental role, for which I am, of course very grateful. But be of good cheer. This little jaunt will be fun and, if nothing else, will allow me to top up my healthy tan and experience some of the culture of Spain.' Bobbie wrinkled her nose. 'If you like, disregarding the expense and increased pressure on my already stretched ex-student's finances, I will call you every couple of days and let you know how I am getting on.'

'I'm sure there will be no need for that ...' said Janet.

'You will call your mother though, won't you?' said Geoff, who would have been happier to have a regular call from Bobbie and slip her a few pounds to cover the expense.

He suspected he would have to make a 'donation' to Bobbie's always-precarious finances anyway nearer the time of her trip, and was expecting her request for funds imminently.

-oo0Ooo-

# Chapter 2

Thursday morning dawned bright and clear and Bobbie, re-arranging her suitcases in the hall once more, was excited.

'Come on, Uncle Geoff! Rosy will be at the station at any moment and we don't have time to waste!'

Geoff, pausing only to kiss Janet as she left for work, was ready with the keys of his Jaguar in his hand.

'Come on then, young Bobbie. Let's go and get her,' he said.

-ooo0oo-

Rosy Brice-Waterman was one of those solid girls who would do well in the light heavyweight class.

She was substantially built and had a laugh like a hyena in a drain, which she deployed at regular intervals.

'Isn't it a scream!' she stated as she swung the heaviest of her cases into the boot of the car with ease. 'I've never been to Spain before, so it will be quite an adventure!'

'You've bought rather a lot of luggage, Rosy,' said Bobbie, 'We will probably have to pay "excess baggage" charges for this lot.'

'Just let them try!' bellowed Rosy, 'It is quite clear on our booking confirmation what we can take. The travel agent chappy told us the maximum weight and that is precisely what I have packed!'

'Ah,' said Bobbie, squeezing into the back seat beside a vast holdall. 'I think I see what has happened here, Rosy. The figure you refer to is the total amount for both of us, and by the look of things, you have snaffled the lot.'

'Oh, I say! Surely not! Blimey, that puts the fox among the pheasants rather.' Rosy turned in her seat to look at Bobbie. 'I'm frightfully sorry, old girl, I may have rather overdone it!'

'Don't worry,' said Geoff. 'If we hurry there is still time to nip home and unpack some of this and start again.'

'Splendid!' shouted Rosy. 'Thank you. I'm not the sort who can holiday with just a bikini and flip-flops, I'm afraid, but I'm sure we can find a solution!'

-ooo0oo-

What they found themselves engaged in, however, when they reached the house was a full-blown row.

In the spare bedroom, with the bathroom scales to hand to weigh the cases, and mountains of clothes on

the two single beds, the floor, and spilling out onto the landing, the girls argued over every garment and as their voices were raised, Geoff left them to it.

'Don't forget we need to leave in an hour, and I'd be grateful if anything you want to leave here was stacked neatly out of the way,' called Geoff over his shoulder as he retreated down the stairs, just as Rosy enquired in a loud voice why Bobbie needed to take quite so many dresses.

The journey to the airport was conducted in a strained silence as the girls sat surrounded by their hastily repacked luggage.

The only comment Bobbie made as they unloaded their cases onto a couple of trollies at the terminal was to the effect that she, Rosy, had to pay any excess baggage charges, which drew a growl but no further comment from the more substantial of the pair.

Having made sure they both had their tickets and passports, Geoff wished them well and made his escape.

-oo0Ooo-

What awaited him back at 2 Easton Drive was something resembling an explosion in a clothing factory.

There were dresses, trousers, tee-shirts, blouses, and even a pair of wellington boots scattered about all over the bedroom.

Geoff was particularly horrified to find a matching tweed jacket and skirt hanging from the lampshade on a coat hanger!

Geoff knew that Janet, whose house this was after all, liked to be tidy and this eruption of clothes cast carelessly around the room would be bound to irritate her, so he started folding up the clothes and positioning them tidily on one of the two beds, Rosy's on the left and Bobbie's on the right.

The process went well initially, as the differences in size made it obvious which belonged to whom, but Geoff felt acutely embarrassed when he came to some of the smaller garments, and he hid four very substantial bras under a tweed jacket on Rosy's bed, and after a moment's indecision two pairs of very brief black lace knickers under a little jacket on Bobbie's.

The process took some time but, topping Rosy's pile off with a copy of Horse and Hound Magazine and Bobbie's with a pair of strappy, cork-heeled sandals that he remembered seeing her wearing, at last it was done. Geoff retired downstairs to catch his breath with a mug of strong coffee.

-oooOoo-

'I think it is a lovely idea to go to Spain for a few days to get to know Orlando,' Janet was saying as they finished their supper. 'I've always wanted to go to that part of the Spanish mainland.'

'Have you?' said Geoff who had long held the opinion that the Costa Blanca was exclusively and entirely Benidorm.

'Yes. Did you know that the highest concentration of Michelin-starred restaurants in the world is there among the lovely little towns where you can buy the catch straight off the fishing boats?' Janet warmed to her theme. 'There are over twenty kilometres of pure sandy beach in one area, dotted with little *chiringuitos*, that means beach bars, by the way, right on the sand for romantic dinners watching the sunset.'

'Amongst the "kiss-me-quick" hats, and Union Jack swimming trunks, a short walk from the British pubs selling all-day breakfasts and fish and chips, I suppose.'

'What? Don't be silly, Geoff. You are muddling that up with somewhere else. The place I'm talking about has a little open-air restaurant on the rocks by the sea where they catch and hang up octopus in the sun to dry, and luxurious, expensive villas overlooking the endless, blue, Mediterranean sea.'

'You've been reading a travel brochure!' exclaimed Geoff.

'Yes. The one Bobbie left behind. The area she is visiting sounds idyllic.'

'Not Benidorm, then.'

'No. Certainly not Benidorm. I think that is on the same stretch of coast line, but it is miles away and nothing to do with the places in Bobbie's brochure.'

'I thought it was all Club 18-30, boozy stag-dos, and that sort of thing.'

'No. I don't think so. Here, take a look for yourself.'

The well-thumbed travel brochure Janet handed him did sing the praises of an area renowned for fine dining, quality wines, and culture as well as stunning beaches and spectacular mountain scenery. Geoff had to admit it looked delightful.

'Don't you think it would be romantic if we took a break from house hunting and went somewhere like that for a week or so, Geoff?'

Geoff, who thought that being anywhere with Janet was the most impossibly romantic thing that had ever happened to him, looked at her smiling face now. That dazzling smile always did it for him.

'Anything I do with you is romantic,' whispered Geoff, swallowing hard. 'I don't need exotic scenery and beautiful locations to take my breath away, Janet. You do that everyday.'

'Have you been drinking?' said Janet, breaking the spell.

'No. Apart from this small beer,' Geoff held up his glass, 'But if you want to go on holiday somewhere like that, I shall be delighted to take you.'

'Really?'

'Certainly.'

Janet moved her chair closer to his.

'And did you mean all that stuff about my taking your breath away?'

'I did,' said Geoff, suddenly feeling very hot, 'I may have mentioned that I love you, Janet, and I simply cannot believe that you even gave me a second glance, let alone invited me to share your life. You are the very best thing that has ever happened to me, and if you can put up with me a little longer, until finances allow, I will take you to watch the sunset in all the exotic locations you like!'

'Oh come here, you soppy old sod!' said Janet, and they left the washing up for the morning.

-ooOoo-

## Chapter 3

The first text message arrived on Janet's phone on the fourth day of Bobbie's holiday.

Janet read it to Geoff over the breakfast table.

'Hi. Sending this to you because I know U.Geoff struggles with anything more technical than a teaspoon, but please read this to him. It is all going very well. We have been to the *Alhambra*, which was amazing, some castles and rather a lot of bars. Orlando is getting on very well with Rosy, which I'm pleased about because I thought he might regard her as a bit of a gooseberry, if that is the fruit I'm thinking of. Rosy studied Economics and Accountancy and they yammer away happily about such delights as Modern Economic Theory and the importance of Re-structure, whatever that is. Tomorrow it's Alicante and another castle, followed by lunch in a three-Michelin-starred restaurant up the coast.
Toodle pip!'

On the sixth day this arrived:-

'We went up to Orlando's villa today. It is gorgeous, but I was surprised to find that he has a Swedish 'live-in' housekeeper. She is tall and blonde and, well, Swedish, and she frisked around him bringing him drinks, and little pastries she made before breakfast, and topping up the paper in his printer and generally being there all the time. They seem to be like an old married couple and I'm going to have to have a talk with him about her. The sea really is the colour of the attached pic. It was taken from one of THREE balconies at his villa, next door to the enormous "infinity" swimming pool. There is even a tennis court and next week, he said, they start laying the base for a helicopter to be able to land! Must close, cocktails are being served.'

The seventh day bought this:-

'Honestly, Rosy sticks to Orlando like a poultice, and rather dominates the conversation with her talk of Economics, Creative Accountancy and what-not. She is becoming a bit of a bore. Orlando seems to lap it up though. I'm finding my specialist subject, "20th Century playwrights and humorists and their effect on contemporary society", is not cutting the intellectual mustard in conversation. I'm beginning to wonder if he had a point when one of my Professors said that my dissertation was 'uncertain and lacking substance'. It is certainly not the conversation starter 'The future of multiple channel accountancy practices' seems to be. Ho Hum.'

Later on the same day Bobbie wrote:-

'Oh cripes, I think it's all going wrong! Orlando and I

had a row about how much time he is spending with Rosy, and he took her side! I've taken myself off to bed in a huff. But just now I looked out of the balcony window and the two of them, Rosy and Orlando, were sitting very close together outside the cocktail bar watching the sunset and yakking away like old comrades.'

The morning of day eight bought a tirade of texts:-

'Rosy didn't come to bed until about half past two this morning. What the hell is she up to?'

'Orlando is not taking my calls. His phone keeps diverting them to answer-phone.'

'Rosy has gone for a long walk. Where the hell is Orlando?'

'It is lunchtime now and still no sign of Rosy and no word from Orlando. I've left him six more messages and the last one was quite pointed.'

'I fell asleep on a sun-lounger by the pool but Pedro, the rather sweet bartender, woke me up with a glass of iced water and suggested I move into the shade. He has sad brown eyes and the longest eyelashes I have ever seen. Still no word from Rosy or Orlando.'

At seven in the evening, Spanish time, this arrived:-

'Rosy's gone! All her stuff has been removed from the room and there was a note saying she was not going to fly back with me, not to worry, and she would explain all later!'

At half past eight:-

'I've just seen Orlando. He has dumped me!'

And five minutes later:-

'Rosy Bovine-Waterspaniel has moved in with Orlando and the Swedish female! Pedro bought me a letter that had been delivered just now. I don't know what to do. I feel so empty and foolish and I can't stop crying.'

Janet replied offering her sympathies, of course, and asking if there was anything be done.

At a little after ten on the morning of day nine Bobbie replied.

'I feel such a little fool. If it wasn't for Pedro, who recently lost his own love, a Swedish girl funnily enough, I think I would just collapse in a heap and wait for the bin men to sweep me up. Thank heavens I'm coming home tomorrow!'

-ooo0oo-

In the car on the way back from the airport, Geoff was surprised to find Bobbie in quite good spirits.
There was not much time for conversation between interruptions from her mobile phone.

'Ah, sweet!' she said, 'Another email from Pedro. He is so nice. He is looking into flights to England if he can get some time off next month. Did I tell you about him, Uncle Geoff? He is really kind and considerate and has these lovely brown eyes. I'm going to take him round in my little sports car and show him all the sights. I can't wait for him to come.'

No need to worry then, Geoff thought. Bobbie had clearly bounced back, and already had a new Spanish chap in tow!

Whatever would she get up to next, Geoff wondered with some alarm.

-oo0Ooo-

# Chapter 4

Pedro's visit, Janet explained, had not been an unalloyed success and Bobbie did not seem to be especially happy with events.

Geoff, returning from a visit to the doctor for a check-up, had awaited the news with interest and not a little concern.

Because of some difficulty she was having with her little sports car, Janet had had to take Pedro back to the airport with Bobbie while Geoff kept his long-standing appointment with the doctor.

'On the way back, she told me she wasn't sure about going out with Pedro again,' explained Janet, 'and while they had had fun, as she put it, the language barrier and certain differences in their backgrounds, made theirs less than a match made in Heaven.'

'Oh dear, poor old Bobbie. Was she very upset?'

'On the contrary,' smiled Janet. 'She seemed rather pleased that the visit was over.'

'Where is she, by the way?' asked Geoff.

'I dropped her at the garage where they are repairing

her car, she should be here at any moment.'

And of course, as she spoke, the unmistakable sound of Bobbie's little sports car coming to an abrupt halt on the gravel outside announced her arrival.

'Brace for impact!' chuckled Geoff.

-oooOoo-

'Hello, Uncle Geoff! Where are we going for dinner?' chirruped Bobbie as she came through the front door, 'Oh, and how did it go at the doctor's? No unusual tropical diseases detected, I trust!'

As usual, the human whirlwind that was Roberta (Bobbie) Bassington filled all the available space with her vivacity.

This irrepressible, often irresponsible but nevertheless enchanting girl seemed bigger than her slight frame would suggest.

Being around Bobbie was always like waiting for something to go bang.

With her long slim legs, turned up nose, dancing red hair and enormous green eyes, Bobbie attracted men with ease, and they seemed to follow her around, for a while at least, like a lovelorn cloud. Then, inevitably, something happened, usually at Bobbie's instigation, and the perfect picture was spoilt.

Bobbie was a one girl explosion looking for somewhere to happen!

-oooOoo-

Bobbie pushed her desert aside.
Not because she didn't want it, or because there was anything wrong with it, but to enable her to spread out a small map on the table in front of her.

'Pedro works in the hotel … here,' she tapped the map with a slim finger, 'The place we went to see was over here, just inland a bit from the sea.'

She traced a line with her finger to a small area on the outskirts of a town and underlined the words "Golf Course" with her fingernail.

'You sort-of look out, round a rather impressive mountain, over the golf course towards the sea, which is here.'

Geoff and Janet craned their necks to see where Bobbie was pointing.

'It's on what they call an "*urbanisation*" in Spain. I think that translates to "housing estate", but don't imagine it is anything like the sour, soulless, suburban sprawl we have in this country. This is something really special, and the locals call it "millionaires mountain" apparently.'

'And this is nothing to do with Orlando, is it?' Geoff asked.

'No, his father's firm just works with the agents who are renting or selling the houses there.' Bobbie replied.

'Good, because after what happened …' frowned Janet.

'Pedro said that the ones which are let out for holidays are managed by an estate agent,' Bobbie explained, 'so it doesn't involve Orlando at all.'

'Although he took you up there?' questioned Geoff.

'Well, yes. But that was only because we were on our way to somewhere else, a Michelin-starred restaurant actually, and he needed to drop off some papers to one of the people who live in one of the mansions up there.'

'Mansions?' said Janet, enthralled.

'Yes. They don't call them that … I've forgotten what they do call them … but there are some pretty massive houses up there with tennis courts and swimming pools and all the fixings.'

'And you say it is possible to rent one of these mansions for a holiday?' asked Geoff.

'So Pedro said. You can even employ staff to bustle about cooking for you, or hand round drinks, or do the ironing or whatever,' explained Bobbie, 'Pedro worked up there once as a pool boy, but ended up tending the poolside bar for some idle rich visitor who demanded "mojitos" every few minutes, delivered to his sun bed.'

'Well, I don't think we could afford anything like that,' said Janet.

'But you don't have to.' Bobbie was tapping the map again. 'Just here, on the same urbanisation, there are a handful of apartments which you can rent for a holiday. Pedro says people stay there to be handy to play golf on the flash course at the bottom of the mountain mostly. But you don't have to be a golfer to rent one.'

'Is that where you took those photos you sent us?' asked Janet.

'Yes. Just opposite there is the whopping great mansion Orlando had to visit, so we took a bit of a wander round while we waited for him and I took those pictures of the view. I was showing them to Pedro when he came over and he recognised where it was and told me about these places you can rent. It's a pretty amazing place actually, that is why I thought you might like to consider taking a short break there.' Bobbie looked from Janet to Geoff and back again. 'And of course if you would like the company of a well-turned-out and rather lovely young woman to add some glamour to the proceedings, I should be able to find a slot in my schedule to accompany you. You could tell the neighbours I was your au-pair or something if you liked.'

Geoff, who had anticipated that Bobbie's motives in mentioning all this were not entirely altruistic, smiled to himself. Janet had expressed great interest in taking a short break from house-hunting and visiting this particular stretch of the Costa Blanca and, although taking Bobbie along had not been part of his vision for their holiday, he had rather warmed to the idea of visiting the area.

Bobbie had passed the map to Janet and turned her attentions once again to her dessert.
Janet was studying the map with interest and had a far-away look in her eyes.

-oo0Ooo-

Two months previously, when Rosy Brice-Waterman left a mountain of clothes strewn about in the spare bedroom at 2 Easton Drive, there was a promise that one of her family would call to collect it all.
At last, today, her younger brother Edmund was due to arrive to collect the items.
They had been placed in dustbin sacks in a corner of the room and Bobbie had needed some persuasion not to drag them out into the garden and burn them.

The hiatus Rosy caused, when she effectively stole Orlando away from Bobbie during their ill-fated trip to Spain, created a rift which showed no sign of healing between the two university friends and since then Bobbie had had no contact at all with Rosy.

Janet tactfully took Bobbie shopping when young Edmund was due to collect the clothing to avoid a confrontation.

Geoff opened the door to a weasel-faced, pencil-thin youth with protruding teeth and a vacant look on his face. The impression was not enhanced by the fact that he stood on the doorstep with his mouth open and waited for Geoff to start the conversation.

'Edmund?' said Geoff.

'Eh?' said the youth, and after a moment's thought, 'I mean yes. What-ho. Come to collect m'sister's clothes and what-not. Edmund Brice-Waterman, brother of the above-mentioned,' and he held out a limp hand for Geoff to shake.

Prudently, Geoff had carried all the dustbin sacks containing Rosy's motley collection of clothing down to the hallway, where they awaited Edmund's arrival.

Without further ado, Geoff helped carry the clothes to a small hatchback, which looked only just big enough for the purpose.

'I say, there is rather a lot more of this than I imagined,' Edmund offered as they pushed and shoved the bags into the cramped space. 'My sister seems to have packed for about a year!'

'Hurmmph!' murmured Geoff into one of the larger sacks and he heaved it into the back seat. 'The sooner this lot is gone the better.'

Sensing a somewhat frosty tone, Edmund hurried to complete packing the car and with a wave said, 'Toodle pip!' and departed.

Geoff, hoping that Bobbie would choose her friends more carefully in future, stomped back into the house and made himself a strong mug of coffee.

-oooOoo-

'There! Did you hear it this time?'

Bobbie was trying to get the mechanic from the garage to identify the noise her little sports car made when turning sharp left.

'Yus, Miss,' replied Gary. 'An' oim pretty sure wot vat is too. Let's go back to va workshop, an' see if oim not roight!'

Trusted with her Uncle Geoff's ageing but pampered Jaguar, this garage, and Gary in particular, was the first port of call for any motoring ailments. It helped, as far as Bobbie was concerned, that Geoff had an account there and bills, issued every three months, might include some minor problem with the little sports car unnoticed, if she was lucky.

Since finishing at Girton College, Cambridge, Bobbie officially lived in Wiltshire with her mother. But she spent a good deal of time with Geoff and Janet, to be, as she put it, 'Closer to the centre of things in London, while I'm looking for a job.'

Bobbie's search for employment was erratic and so far, unproductive, and she knew that she had to do better than the half-hearted attempts to find work she had undertaken so far. But her somewhat vague idea of what she wanted to do was at odds with her strong determination to wring every ounce of fun and mischief out of life before her golden youth passed by. She also knew that she could manipulate boys, and never failed to tease, flirt and enchant, when those that attracted her came along.

Gary did not fit that model by a long measure.

Forty, short and paunchy, with three days' growth of grimy stubble and a balding head, he was nevertheless much taken with Bobbie and was always happy to attend to her and the temperamental little car she drove, whenever the chance arose.

He spent longer looking at her shapely, tanned legs than was strictly necessary, as the dress she wore sitting in the passenger seat of the car rode up slightly, and some rapid re-adjustment of the steering was called for as they careered around a bend near the garage.

As it was a left turn, there was the noise again, and Gary covered his lascivious behaviour by saying, 'Yus. Just as oi suspeck. It'll be a stone stuck in the brakes, thas wot!'

With the car back on the ramp the problem was soon resolved and somewhat reluctantly, as he lowered it to the ground, Gary had to say goodbye.

'Spec yew'd loik me ta put this on yer uncle's account, Miss Bobbie,' he said wisely, as with a wave and a smile, Bobbie roared off into the throbbing heart of the leafy Hampshire suburb Geoff and Janet called home.

-ooOoo-

## Chapter 5

Of course, the programme for the short holiday did not include Bobbie to start with, but she explained that if she was allowed to tag along, she could see if there was, after all, any future for a relationship between her and Pedro, which she referred to as "unfinished business".

'You ought to look for a job as some sort of salesman, Bobbie,' said Geoff as Janet left for work. 'The way you twisted Janet round your little finger was disgraceful.'

'Oh, Uncle Geoff! You don't think so really do you? About my selling the idea to Janet, I mean?' Bobbie's smirk was unmistakable, 'I'm so fond of Janet, and I just want the best for you both. You will hardly notice that I'm there, except perhaps on occasional evenings when, as Janet said, maybe we can make up a foursome for romantic dinners with Pedro.'

'You are a shameless minx, Bobbie,' said Geoff, grinning in spite of himself.

'Well, that's what salesmen do, isn't it? Perhaps I will peruse the job pages for something along those lines, where they might appreciate the addition of a little class and decorative elegance to their otherwise no-doubt tawdry sales workforce. I wonder if there are openings for staff selling fast sports cars to the seriously wealthy, or perhaps some involvement in the world of the better sort of jewellery and diamonds calls?'

'Stop it, you cheeky monkey, or I'll tell your mother that you put the repairs for your car on my account at the garage!' Geoff smiled.

'Ah. You found out about that, did you?'
Bobbie again showed no remorse and brazened it out.
'Well, I was caught on the horns of a dilemma, Uncle Geoff. You see the car may actually have been dangerous and a certain fiscal unpleasantness was inevitable, had I had to own up that I hadn't actually got a bean. So, when Gary suggested popping it on the old account I knew you would rather your favourite niece-by-marriage was driving a safe dear little sports car and not taking a risk.' Bobbie hardly paused for breath,
'So for now, until finances improve, I took up his idea.' Bobbie unleashed one her most charming smiles and fluttered her eyelashes. 'And who knows, if I get a job as a salesman, or should that be "salesperson" in these enlightened times, no doubt the commission will soon start to flow and I can pay you back with interest.'

-ooo0oo-

Their trip in the clammy taxi to the airport was

conducted in a sort of miasma or fug of old cigarettes, drunks, sweat and dirty windows, which refused to open beyond the merest crack.

'Uggg!' exclaimed Janet as they arrived at the terminal, 'I hope we don't get him on the way back as well. I feel as if I need a shower!'

'I managed not to be sick,' said Bobbie, 'But it was close!'

'There must be some sort of rule he is breaking by using a taxi in that condition. I'm feeling distinctly itchy,' Geoff added to the mood of unhappy disapproval. 'And its not as if he was cheap!'

'Passport ready, Bobbie?' said Janet.

'Yup. All set!'

'Right then. Sunny Spain, here we come!'

-oo0Ooo-

It didn't smell like the revolting taxi, but Pedro's elderly and very battered car had certainly been around the block a few times.

'Isn't he pretty,' whispered Bobbie to Janet as he put the cases in the boot at the airport, 'Those eyelashes!'

'These old Opels are not far off classic car status now,' said Geoff, looking at the faded and peeling paintwork. 'There are so few left, and the Vauxhall version we have in England is now seriously rare.'

'Lo siento. I'm a sorry. I no think I follow ..' said Pedro.

'Uncle Geoff says he likes your car,' added Bobbie helpfully.

-ooOoo-

There was no question about it, the view from the terrace at the rear of the holiday apartment was terrific.

Looking past the pristine golf course, to the right, was a towering and impressive mountain peak and straight ahead, a splendid view of the sea.

'The estate agent said that island you can see over there is Ibiza,' said Janet. 'Isn't it gorgeous!'

'No es Ibiza,' said Pedro, lifting in the last of the cases, 'Ees Callera, down a the coast near Oliva and Valencia.'

'Well, it's very pretty, anyway,' Janet stated as she rested her elbows on the parapet of the balcony terrace, drinking in the view.

'I told you it was brilliant,' said Bobbie, 'Now Pedro, where are we going for supper?'

'I sorry. I no have money for the supper, and tonight I'm a have to work.' Pedro looked embarrassed.

'Oh, don't worry about the money side of things, Pedro,' said Bobbie, drawing him aside out of earshot, 'Uncle Geoff is always good about that sort of thing and I'm sure he will cough up when required.'

'He is a ill?' Pedro looked concerned.

'No, sweetie. I mean he will cough up the money .. pay for things. Understand?'

'Oh, yays, I see. He is a … how you say? Money-bags?'

'Well, I wouldn't put it quite like that, but he can usually be relied on to pay, especially where his favourite niece-by-marriage is concerned … that's me by the way.'

'You haf a furry nice family, Bobbie. They very good peoples.'

'Yes,' said Bobbie, looking at Pedro with her head on one side in an appraising way, 'And you are a very nice peoples to.' And with that she kissed him on the cheek and patted his bottom as she gently propelled him out of the door. 'See you tomorrow.'

-ooOOoo-

Geoff was enchanted.

His view of the Costa Blanca had been a jaundiced and out-of-date version of something which might have existed in the early 1970s.

As a youth, his parents had sneered at the idea of package holidays in places like Benidorm and Torremolinos, where they believed the worst sort of British workers let their hair down and behaved disgracefully.

They followed the popular view that Spanish food was likely to be cooked in engine oil and the hotels by the coast were all cockroach-infested flea-pits, which were infrequently cleaned and served by unreliable sanitation.

His family spent their vacations taking improving walks in the Lake District or Scottish Highlands and the nearest he got to a trip overseas was a fortnight in a caravan on the Isle of Wight.

Since reaching man's estate Geoff had broadened his horizons and had visited Italy, Greece, America and even parts of Africa, but he had studiously avoided Spain as the outdated views of his parents still lingered.

What lay before him now, however, was a revelation.

Quite apart form the stunning scenery of the Northern Costa Blanca, the food they ate in restaurants was of the very highest quality and when they 'self catered', Pedro took them to a colourful market where he helped them to buy the freshest vegetables and best cuts of meat to cook on the little barbecue, helpfully provided on the terrace, where they could watch spectacular sunsets over the sea.

'I've never had such tasty vegetables,' Janet declared at one point, 'and it's all so fresh and clean.'

'Well, you don't think they send the best stuff to England, do you?' said Bobbie, 'They keep that here for their own use!'

'I do believe you are right, Bobbie,' said Geoff, 'These carrots actually taste like carrots, and the lettuce is so crisp and fresh, it is difficult to believe we put up with the rubbish they serve up in British supermarkets. Compared to this, the stuff we get is little better than what the Spanish throw away!'

'We only like a fresh,' said Pedro, 'No like a, how you say, reservists?'

'Preservatives,' corrected Bobbie with a smile.

'Si. Is why the bread, he must a be bought every day. He no keep nice. He pretty soon get mouldy like the English.'

'I think he means the English bread,' suggested Bobbie.

'Si. No keep a Spanish in the fridge for a week. The Spanish he always fresh!'

'Yes, I think we see,' said Janet, chuckling quietly.

-oooOoo-

The day had arrived when Bobbie intended to put her plan into action.

They sat in Pedro's car a little way down the narrow road with a good view of their target.

'You a really sure about this, Bobbie,' said Pedro, expressing again the doubts he had about the entire scheme.

'Yes. I am sure it will be fine,' said Bobbie, touching his cheek. 'If you know how the controls work we will be in and out in five minutes and can sit up there on that hill and watch as they rush about wondering what to do!'

Si. Is furry funny, but yes, no. What if a we caught?'

'Who on earth is going to catch us out here, sweetheart? It must be half a mile, I mean a kilometre, to the nearest house and there is nobody about.'

'But the Ingrid, she is about, and a maybe the Orlando too.'

'But that is the whole point, you sweet boy. They won't have a clue what to do and it will serve them right for the way they treated us both!'

'Bobbie,' Pedro said now, looking at her through lowered eyelids, 'I a think you are furry crazy girl, but I liking you a whole lot.'

'More than you liked Ingrid?'

'Yays. I'm thinking even more than I once a like Ingrid. You lovely, Bobbie.'

A few moments later, a very well-kissed Bobbie sighed, gently pushed Pedro away, and said something to the effect that it was time to put the plan into action.

They left the car and, keeping the in shade of the row

of palms in front of the house to hide them from view, they stole along the track below the huge villa.

Pedro, who held a large blue wrench in his hand, helped Bobbie through a gap in the hedge and they climbed carefully up the steep stony slope towards the house.

Now below the base of the infinity pool, on a raised area facing the sea, they paused to check their bearings.

Pedro pointed with the wrench to a small steel door set in the concrete wall below the pool, but as they approached it, they both froze when the unmistakable sound of someone diving into the pool just above their heads broke the silence.

'Somebody is a …' whispered Pedro.

'Yes, I know, but the noise they make in the water will cover us. Go!' whispered Bobbie.

With a gulp, Pedro, realising that despite his misgivings he now had no choice, stepped up to the steel door and turned the handle.

-ooo0oo-

Geoff and Janet spent the day pottering around the little artisan shops near the beach and enjoying lunch in a *chiringuito* right on the sand.

'It's nice that Bobbie and Pedro seem to be getting on so well,' said Janet, 'He seems very sweet.'

'It's always the nice ones that Bobbie seems to mess about in some way and loose,' said Geoff.

'Oh, don't be so hard on her, Geoff. She is still very young and at least she tries.'

'Yes. She can be very trying, just ask her mother!'

'Oh, very funny!' Janet pulled face. 'What do you think they are doing now?'

'The same as us, I should think. Spending my money in a bar somewhere.'

'You old sourpuss! You know full well you spoil Bobbie and love doing it!'

'All right, your honour, I admit all the charges. It's always been like that for me with Bobbie since she was very little and lost her father. She might have her moments but she is essentially a delightful girl who would never do anything to upset anyone deliberately.'

'Of course she wouldn't,' said Janet.

-ooOoo-

At that moment Bobbie was doing something to deliberately upset her former boyfriend, Orlando, and his 'live-in Swedish housekeeper', Ingrid, who just happened to be Pedro's ex-girlfriend.

Together they manhandled the wide, blue, flexible plastic tube onto the pipe and tightened the flange, then Pedro attached the wrench to the large nut, which was painted red, under the warning notice.

'Choo ready?' he said.

'Let's do it!' whispered Bobbie.

Needing no further encouragement, Pedro gave the red painted nut a determined twist in the anti-clockwise direction, and with a groan the valve began to open.

'That's it! Run!' said Pedro, but Bobbie was already at the door and starting to scramble down the scree to the road.
Pedro dropped the wrench and hared after her as fast as his legs would carry him.

-ooOOoo-

'Isn't this romantic!' Janet was saying. 'In a place like this you really do feel that nothing can go wrong and all is right with the world.'

'The bill, please,' said Geoff, forgetting for a moment that he had promised to try to use the handful of little Spanish phrases Janet had been teaching them both for their holiday.

'It is lovely and peaceful, isn't it,' said Geoff, looking out to sea. 'I could stay here like this forever.'

-ooOOoo-

From their vantage point, some distance above the

villa, concealed behind some bins and a tall tree beside the rough stone road, and now back in the old car, Bobbie and Pedro watched as the scene of domestic chaos unfolded below them.

Ingrid, completely naked with her long blonde hair sticking to her wet body, was rushing from one side of the infinity pool to the other and screaming for Orlando.

She cast increasingly anxious glances alternately downwards, at the gushing, bubbling torrent of water spewing out onto the little road, the vortex of swirling water in the pool by the emergency drain, and at the slow but inevitably dropping water level.

At last she was joined by Orlando, still clutching his mobile phone and dressed in a business suit, who was also shouting and waving his free arm about.

Pedro and Bobbie were too far away to hear what they were saying, although the sound of the rushing splashing water would have made it impossible to hear them unless they were very much closer.

Pedro had thought to bring a small set of binoculars with him and he now had these in his hand. When he sighed, Bobbie noticed that he was focussing on Ingrid's naked form through them.

She nudged him none to gently in the ribs and said 'Hoy!'

'Whoops. I sorry Bobbie. But she a does have a furry

nice ….'

'Yes, well never mind that,' said Bobbie, snatching the binoculars away from him. 'There is Orlando and there is Ingrid, but there doesn't seem to be anyone else there.'

By this stage Orlando was trying to climb down through the bushes to the steel door behind which the pool mechanism lay. To get to it he would have to pass through the powerful torrent of water which was erupting from it, and as he got closer he hesitated as it became clear the task was dangerous and impossible.

Ingrid, meanwhile, was standing, still naked, on the side of the pool and shouting into a mobile phone, no doubt summoning help.

'It's just the two of them,' said Bobbie. 'There is nobody else there.'

Pedro looked. It was just the two of them. Naked Ingrid and Orlando in his soaking business suit.

'Is only them, si. You think a there should be someone more?'

'Yes,' said Bobbie. 'I was hoping Rosy Brice-Waterman would be there too.'

'You don't a know?,' said Pedro. 'She go back England after one week. No say why.
Please you tell me, what meaning is "threesacrowd"?'

At that moment they heard the distinctive siren of

the Bomberos, the Spanish fire service, and Pedro said that it was time they moved.

-ooOoo-

# Chapter 6

**Spain:**

Orlando's flight from the UK was delayed and his father, already very red, turned a deeper hue as he finished the call from his son and turned on his heel to walk back towards the villa, where the Mayor, various officials and the digger driver awaited.

His rage at his son for ignoring the warning signs and believing that the Town Hall had no intention of carrying out its threat to knock down the illegally-built villa would have to be vented at some future point.

For now he had to find a way to buy time as they searched for a way to stop the Town Hall's men from carrying out their threatened demolition of the large, luxurious villa where Orlando and Ingrid lived. But he was running out of ideas as well as time.

**Three months earlier: England - Wiltshire:**

After the hiatus Rosy Brice-Waterman caused in Spain, it was not a surprise that Bobbie wanted nothing more to do with her, but the revelation that she had returned to England within days of Bobbie's own departure did give her pause for thought.

Undoubtedly, Orlando had behaved disgracefully, and Rosy had taken full advantage of the attraction he apparently felt for her. But then there was the situation with Ingrid, the 'live-in Swedish housekeeper'. Was she somehow involved in Rosy's rapid return home?

In amongst all this uncertainty Bobbie did wonder if Orlando had hurt Rosy too.

At the end of her latest trip to Spain with Geoff and Janet, after which Bobbie found herself to be missing Pedro quite a lot more than she expected, she had wondered again what Rosy might be feeling and how she had extracted herself from Orlando's no-doubt tangled arrangements.

That was soon resolved when a letter arrived at Matravers Hall, and finding it on the hall-stand, Bobbie picked it up.

The letter had been delivered when Bobbie was actually in Spain, but had been left on the hall stand for her return.

Bobbie collected it and carried it with her luggage up to the Blue Room, which she always regarded as her personal domain when in her mother's house.

The letter, cast onto the sofa in the sitting area of the Blue Room suite, caught Bobbie's eye after she had unpacked and showered. She opened it and sat down to read the contents.

"Now obviously you hate me, and that is

understandable," it started. "But before you burn this letter, please, for old times' sake if nothing else, do read it to the end."

Bobbie felt her hackles rise as she realised the letter was from Rosy Brice-Waterman and represented the first contact the two former university friends had had since the awfulness in Spain.

Her first inclination was to cast the letter from her, prior to burning it as Rosy suggested, but her wiser self realised that it must have taken some emotional toll to put pen to paper like this and she decided to read on.

"You and I have both been the playthings of the most awful and manipulative man that ever drew breath, and to say I regret what happened is to understate the situation by the widest margin.
I have wronged you, Bobbie, and my heart is broken into a thousand pieces by that fact alone, but I was also misled and while you may well say that served me right, I simply cannot just leave it at that.
I do not deserve your forgiveness, but you do deserve the truth, so, painful though it may be here it comes…

"Orlando offered me an 'opportunity' in which he expected me to use my knowledge of advanced company accountancy theory to help him set up a complete new accounting system for his law practice and to build into it a method whereby he could quietly skim off an element of the profits to send to certain clandestine bank accounts he operates.

In return, he offered me a full-time job in his London office when it was done and a quite substantial cash incentive up-front to step in with his plans.

He also made me sign a 'confidentiality agreement' (in three different languages) and made it clear that if I did not do as he wanted things would go badly for me.

"You probably thought that he was interested in me romantically, and for a very short while, to my eternal shame, so did I, but that was not to be. What Orlando wanted was an untraceable way to filch money from his father's firm to feed his playboy lifestyle around the world.

"He led me to believe that he would finish with you so that we could be together and I'm sorry to say that, at that point, I believed him. But then I discovered that Ingrid is not his 'live-in Swedish housekeeper', she is his fiancé!

"When I found that out I extracted myself and booked a flight home. I had to leave most of my possessions there and walk miles to the nearest village to do it, but at least I was able to escape.

When he realised I had gone, Orlando sent me a text which made out that I approached him and tried to get him to do illegal things with his company accounts and that if he ever saw me again he would have me arrested.

"He was just covering his back of course, but it hurt nonetheless. I also found out that Ingrid got engaged to him about three months before we got to Spain.

It seems Orlando is not bothered about being faithful though, and leading you on and not telling the truth about Ingrid was reprehensible. You will wonder, no doubt, how he had the nerve to take us up to his house, but it seems he told Ingrid we were there so he could talk business with me!
I was horrified when I found out the true situation and could not wait to get away.

"Ingrid is also not all she seems. I was only able to spend limited time with her, but it was quickly clear that she is a gold-digger with a past. Orlando told me quite shamelessly that he met her when he 'hired' her as an escort, whatever that might mean, and when she realised the set-up and how rich he was, I suspect she stuck to him like glue. They plan to get married next April.
She was also quite unpleasant to me when I asked about their relationship.

"So the reality is that we have both had a narrow escape from something really quite nasty, and although I can appreciate that you might never be able to talk to me again, I do hope that you now can understand the situation and that you know that I only wish you all the very best.
I also wish with every fibre of my being that none of this had ever happened and that we could return to how things were.
Now that I know that horrible creatures like Orlando exist in the world, I shall probably never trust anyone again. But my greatest regret is losing you as my best

friend.

I hope things work out well for you, Bobbie, and that this experience will not dim the flame of your splendid effervescent nature.

With the deepest and most heartfelt sorrow.

Rosy."

## England - London:

There was to be a meeting that morning between some people from the tax office next door and Mike's boss, amongst others.

Mike should have been there but with Rosalind's pregnancy steadily progressing and his benign employer allowing husbands to attend occasional anti-natal classes with their wives, he was not at his desk. Working for the Civil Service had its compensations and the office of the Department for International Trade, where Mike earned his salary, treated their staff well where family matters were concerned.

As he sat on the almost empty mid-morning train on his way to the office after the class, Mike's thoughts turned to work once more and he wondered what the unusual meeting was all about.

All he knew was that it involved an investigation into a big international law firm. His office had helped them to set up a London headquarters.

That was under a now-defunct multi-departmental Government initiative to encourage foreign professional services companies to come and invest in the UK and employ and train a percentage of British staff in their businesses.

The scheme had been managed by Mike's department and he himself had worked on an element of the project some time ago. He couldn't see that much could have gone wrong with the scheme after all this time, so he looked forward to getting to the office and learning what it was all about.

**England - Suburban Hampshire/Surrey borders:-**

'It was very upsetting, Janet,' said Geoff.

'Oh, poor Bobbie. It is just one thing after another for her, isn't it.' Janet reached out and gently squeezed Geoff's hand.

'She read me the whole letter, in between sniffs and snivels, and asked if she could come up and see us for the weekend.'

'Yes, of course. If Bobbie wants to come, that's fine.' Janet looked concerned. 'Thank goodness she didn't get too far involved with this Orlando, although I do feel a bit sorry for Rosy too.'

Janet frowned as she thought more about the situation.

'She should not have encouraged him. Mind you, as it turned out, it is just as well that she did, because it stopped poor Bobbie getting in too deep.'

'I hadn't thought of that,' said Geoff, 'But you are right, of course. In a sense, although this is an awful thing to say, because of what Rosy did, Bobbie was saved from deeper involvement.'

At that point Geoff's mobile phone rang, and a glance at the screen told him it was Bobbie calling.

-ooo0oo-

## Chapter 7

'Yays,' said Pedro, 'It was furry funny. Is most a funny thing happen ever. Still I laughing!'

'Good gracious, Bobbie,' Geoff exclaimed. 'Whatever where you thinking! Supposing you had been caught!'

At last it had come out that Bobbie and Pedro had mischievously let all the water out of the pool at Orlando's villa in revenge for how he had treated them.

'Oh, Uncle Geoff, honestly. The villa was at least half a mile from anything, right out in the countryside. There was no chance of even the most observant and unnaturally long-sighted person spotting us.'

'Yays, he is right out in the *campo*, on the side of the big hill, with just a the lane leading there only. He furry quiet there,' smiled Pedro on the 'FaceTime' screen on Bobbie's iPad.

'I think letting the water out of the pool like that was deeply irresponsible of you both!' said Geoff.

Janet, meanwhile, could contain her laughter no longer and had to get up and go into the kitchen.

'So, Pedro, sweetie,' Bobbie was saying now, 'How much paid holiday have you got left you take. You know how much I want to see you …'

'Is a not the holiday. I got plenty, been working furry hard. Is dinero, I mean money. I saving and a saving but not still I got enough for the plane to England. Is very 'spensive.'

'Oh, Pedro, then when am I going to see you again?' whined Bobbie.

'No, Geoff,' said Janet eyeing him as she returned from the kitchen, 'There has to be a limit.'

'But, Janet, Bobbie has some savings and with just a small loan …'

'You are dreadful,' said Janet, taking charge, 'Bobbie, how much does Pedro need to come over for a week?'

'Que?' said Pedro, from the FaceTime screen, 'What you say?'

And so it was decided. Geoff would meet Pedro at the airport while Bobbie attended an interview for a job as an "advertising sales executive" for a local radio station, in two weeks' time.

-oooOoo-

The limited 'stay of execution' Orlando's father had managed, with some difficulty to negotiate, did not give them long.

The completely spurious reasons he offered the Mayor and the council workers not to proceed with the demolition would soon be revealed as untrue. Ingrid was not pregnant and all too soon that fact would emerge.

-oooOoo-

Rosalind, however, was very pregnant indeed and was finding it difficult to do much of anything.

Until a week ago she had been painting skirting boards and arranging and rearranging furniture in the nursery they were preparing for the new arrival, but now she found any physical activity too much.

She and Mike had agreed that they did not want to know the sex of the baby before it was born and they had stuck to their plan, although it caused some difficulties in choosing colours for the nursery, which was now mostly white with a touch of trendy russet brown, and with friends and relatives wanting to buy gifts.

They reasoned that the baby would spend some weeks in a cot in their bedroom so they had plenty of time to add appropriate colours and touches to the nursery, and could buy the inevitable pink or blue clothes when the need arose.

Although she had longed to be pregnant for several difficult years before it happened, Rosalind was fed up with it now and couldn't wait for it to be over.

Her friend, Helen, who was bustling about in the kitchen popped her head round the door.

'All right in there, mummy?' she chirruped, 'The casserole is all set and on now. Would you like another cup of tea?'

'Oh, thank you, Helen, I really do appreciate this,' Rosalind replied.

'No problem. You know I love to cook and whistling up a casserole doesn't take long. At least it saves you having to worry about feeding Mike when he gets home. Now then, mummy, what about that tea?'

'I wish you wouldn't call me mummy,' said Rosalind, 'I'm not one yet, after all.'

'But it is only a matter of days now until you are and I told you, I've been reading that the baby can hear us talking. I want my godchild to know that you are called "mummy" from the outset, and Rosalind is a bit of a mouthful for a new born!'

The two friends laughed and, sitting as comfortably as they could in the circumstances, on the big beanbags on the floor, drank their tea.

-ooo0oo-

After the accident with the pool water escaping, which Orlando was still convinced was a deliberate act caused by persons unknown, life for Ingrid had taken on an uncomfortable feeling of uncertainty.

The *Bomberos*, the Spanish fire service, had taken some hours to completely stem the flow of gushing chlorinated water from the broken valve, and the track at the bottom of the now almost-empty infinity pool had all but washed away.

There had been concerns too that the chlorinated water could damage the vines in the adjacent field and make the grapes unsaleable, and the farmer's complaints had alerted the Town Hall to what had happened.

Since then the place had been crawling with officials.

Surveyors came and went, as did grim-faced people from the local Council and even the police.

Ingrid missed her twice-daily swims and lazy days by the pool sunbathing and looking out at the amazing view of the sea from a choice of three terraces that the elevated luxurious villa provided.

She had confidence that matters would return to normal soon, however, and with good reason. Orlando's father's legal firm had a formidable reputation and it would not be long before they found a way to remove this ludicrous threat of demolition, she was sure.

After all, she reasoned, there were hundreds of villas built illegally in the *campo*, or countryside. Most had permission only for a small hut as a farm shelter or for a goatherd to stay in, and living permanently there was not usually allowed. But that had not stopped dozens of them being developed and extended or replaced with large houses over the years. What did one more of those matter, and what harm was the isolated villa doing anyway?

The Town Hall obviously either didn't know it was there or, until the incident with the pool and the farmer's complaints forced it into the limelight, chose to turn a blind eye. Now, however, they were threatening to exercise their powers and actually knock the illegally-built villa down.

Ingrid liked her life to be nice and smooth and calm, and she liked her little luxuries. She also meant to ensure that that was exactly what she got, if Orlando knew what was good for him.

-oo0Ooo-

'I will even get a firm's car after a year if it all works out,' enthused Bobbie. 'Although unfortunately it will have "XBS radio. Your local station for news and sport, traffic, weather and music 24 hours a day" written all down the side of it. I saw three of them in the car park painted up like that. Still, a free car is not to be sneezed at, is it?!'

'Well, that does sound good,' said Janet. 'I must tune in to this XBS radio and see what it is all about.'

'I had a listen to it yesterday in the car, when Bobbie went for the interview and I was on my way to the airport,' said Geoff. 'It is one of those commercial radio stations were the news gets interrupted by adverts every two minutes and even the weather is sponsored by some local brewery.'

'Oh, but that is the whole point, Uncle Geoff! It will be my job to find new advertisers and keep the ones they already have happy with special offers and what-have-you,' smiled Bobbie, 'So the more advertisers there are the better!'

'So,' said Pedro, 'You go to these a people and say "Put you advert on el radio with us and I getting the commission," yays?'

'Something like that, although I shall be learning the actual sales patter from someone called Lindsay who will be taking me round to see how it is done to start with. After that I dare say I shall develop my own methods to impress the adoring customers and when I present them with the chance to deal with someone with my easy self-assured elegance and charm, no doubt sales will increase steadily.'

'Don't be too cocky, young lady,' Geoff said. 'Sales jobs can be really hard work, especially when you constantly have to find new customers. And you probably will have to, if as you say, you will get paid just a small basic salary and then mostly commission.'

'Well, I'm just delighted that you have got a job,

Bobbie, and I'm sure you will do your best and make a success of it,'

Janet treated her to a radiant smile.

'Thank you, Janet. It is good to know I have your support, especially as I shall have to be living here until I can afford a place of my own.'

'Ay?!' said Geoff.

-ooOoo-

## Chapter 8

'So you knew that Ingrid worked as an escort then, Pedro?'

'Yays, but she not do that till after we split up. She work at the hotel then.'

Bobbie studied Pedro's face. It was so good to have him here, but she could not help wanting to know more about Ingrid and although his relationship with her was history, she still felt irrational pangs of jealousy.

'What did she do at the hotel, then?' she asked.

Pedro chuckled. 'Well, not a much mostly! She lazy girl. She supposed to be cocktail waitress but she a like sunbathing with the guests. That's a how she meet the Victor.'

'Victor?' asked Bobbie.

'Yays. He nasty … how you say? … pieceashit? He running the massage parlours in the town and they say he own the two biggest clubs too.'

'What? A nightclub owner, you mean?'

'Eh, not sactly, Bobbie. In Espana, when we say "club"

we not mean like Eenglish.'

'Well, what do you mean then?'

'Umm … They not furry nice places, Bobbie. They where men go and pay the girls …'

With a sharp intake of breath, Bobbie said, 'Oh, I see! Ingrid didn't work in one of those, did she?'

'No, no! Not a like a that! No, the Ingrid she nice girl. Furry posh. She went to the good eschool, speaka many language. When she leave the hotel and a finish me, she go to the Victor and work as high-class person who go to work with the businessmen. That how she meet the Orlando.'

'This Victor introduced her to Orlando?'

'Yays. She furry clever girl and Orlando, he no speaks the Italian.'

'I don't understand?' Bobbie scratched her head, 'What has speaking Italian got to do with it?'

'Is why she escort for the Orlando.' Pedro looked a Bobbie askance, 'You no think …'

'What?'

Pedro was laughing now.

'I think this big, how you say … misunderstand? The Ingrid she fly to the Rome with the Orlando to do the business there. She the escort for the talking Italian. That her new job.'

'Oh gosh!' All the air left Bobbie's body in a rush. 'You mean she is an interpreter!'

'Interpreter? Si, yes. She the escort of Orlando do the speak Italian.'

'I think I'd better explain to you what "escort" can also mean in English, Pedro. You are so adorable!'

Pedro looked confused as Bobbie laughed out loud, but he understood "adorable" and he liked that.

-oooOoo-

'Oh, that's all fixed up.' said Janet. 'Bobbie will move in here when she starts her new job, just temporarily'.

'But what about when we move house? And how long will this go on for?' Geoff asked incredulously.

'Oh, don't worry, Geoff, it will all sort itself out. I thought you would be pleased I had offered to help Bobbie out.'

'But you don't know what she is like!' Geoff exclaimed, 'If she isn't under any deadline to move out we could be stuck with her for years!'

'Oh, I'm sure nothing like that will happen. Bobbie said she is already talking to someone at the radio station about renting a bedsit or something in her house.'

'Oh, glory! I can just see this ending in disaster. And

we all know who will have to pick up the pieces!' Geoff was on his way to the kitchen to make himself a strong cup of tea to help get over the shock.

-oo0Ooo-

Rosalind's labour started shortly after Mike finished the meeting with his boss, and in a blizzard of panicky phone calls Mike broke his own rule and took a taxi to the station.

Mike and Rosalind had organised everything carefully, with Rosalind's bag packed and waiting in the hall. But despite being ready, nobody is ever really prepared for the arrival of a first-born.

Rosalind's mother, who lived in Cambridge, was in the same railway station at the same time as Mike, although on different trains, so they didn't actually meet. But both were headed for the same address with a mix of nervousness and excitement.

Her friend Helen asked to leave work early when Rosalind's text arrived and was the first to arrive at the house, but she was still twenty minutes after the taxi had left to take Rosalind the short journey to the local hospital who, by then, were expecting her.

Helen, who had had a key to the house cut to cover just such an event, headed for the kitchen as planned. She knew that when anything actually happened at the hospital she could get there quickly enough, but that a wait was inevitable, so she settled in to create, batch cook and freeze a selection of tasty meals for Mike to warm up as necessary.

The plan was coming together and Rosalind would not be on her own for long.

-oooOoo-

The wastepaper basket was already half full.

Bobbie had tried writing the letter on her iPad, as an email, but decided it need to be drafted on paper and it was not proving easy to do, however hard she tried.

She had come up with a couple of good sentences which she wrote out in the back of her notebook to be included later in the final version, but she could not work out how to start or finish the letter.

The problem was that she was really not sure whether she did, or did not, want to see Rosy Brice-Waterman again, after all.

The two had been great friends at university and shared that horizon-expanding experience together, helping each other out when the need arose, and enjoying each others' company, but now that she came to think about it, what else did they have in common?

Rosy came from a big, wealthy family and grew up in some style in a rambling country house surrounded by her horses, dogs, cats and acres of prime Shropshire farmland. Her family even had staff, including gardeners, grooms, a gamekeeper, and as a piece of living history seemingly from another era, an elderly and imperious butler, who regarded the young visiting Bobbie with apparent disapproval in that particular way that only butlers can, and peered at her through old-fashioned glasses with his gooseberry eyes.

Rosy sailed through her exams and graduated with ease, whilst Bobbie struggled to get to grips with her chosen studies into '20th Century humorists', who seemed to slip through her fingers like spindrift.

Rosy's home life seemed to be one long round of horse riding, amateur rowing events, local charity work and trying to duck out of the endless routine of dinners, dances, and society get togethers her family wanted to involve her in.

She was large, boisterous and noisy and while she was great fun to be with most of the time, her outdoorsy, breezy 'all for it' attitude could be quite exhausting after a while.

Bobbie's family had lived in some style once too, before she was born. But now Matravers Hall had been divided up into five, admittedly quite substantial, 'wings' and two flats. Since her father died and for as long as she could remember her home had been one of those 'wings', rather than the entire estate.

Her mother's writing kept the wolf from the door, now that it was just the two of them, but when Bobbie was small there had been a period when she had to hold down two jobs to keep her daughter in her private school and she had to work long into the night on her novels to make ends meet.

Although widowed quite young, her mother had never remarried and now, in her late fifties, she buried herself in her books.

She had a sister, Bobbie's aunt and Geoff's ex-wife, who she was close to, and Uncle Geoff, as she called him, had been a permanent feature of Bobbie's life since she was eight years old.

Bobbie's natural effervescence was allowed to bloom unfettered in the quiet surroundings of Matravers Hall, but inevitably its confines soon became too restricting as she grew up.

She didn't have many really close friends apart from Rosy, although she collected acquaintances continually, and was always popular with boys.

That, and the fact that this latest hiatus had come between them, left Bobbie unprepared for how to deal with the situation she found herself in now.

As another draft was screwed up and thrown into the wastepaper basket, Bobbie felt the tears start in her eyes and buried her face in her hands.

-oooOoo-

It had been a bruising interview, and no less so

because it was conducted over a mobile phone, rather than face to face.

Orlando's father never minced his words, but the tirade he delivered to his son now exceeded all past records.

The trouble was, mused Orlando, that he was right, and there was no getting around it.

When Kurt, the arrogant, bombastic, German born-builder found backers and became an international property developer, he started building houses and flats all over Europe. Orlando's father hung onto his coat tails and secured all of the legal work he had to offer.
Kurt became their most important client as well as a friend of the family.

The relationship, however, was certainly not one-sided and Kurt benefitted greatly from all the specialist taxation advice, planning expertise and contact sharing that the lawyers and their associates provided.

These symbiotic arrangements they developed over the years made Orlando's father rich, and as a result anything Kurt wanted, he got.

Kurt had repaid the trust they had built up handsomely over the years, however, and not long ago he had bought the land and built the villa that Orlando and Ingrid lived in now, and handed it over to them as a token of his appreciation.

Orlando's father stayed close to Kurt as much as their diverse business interests allowed, and they had recently visited the Bentley showroom in London together to take delivery of almost identical cars. An imposing two-door model stood outside the villa now, as a furious Kurt argued with the young female architect who had designed the place and a cowering official from the Town Hall about the legality of the situation.

Orlando hovered to one side, unwilling, and for the moment unable to enter into the debate. His ear still rang from the explosion of vitriol he had received by mobile phone from his father, and the more he thought about it, the more hard-done-by he felt.

Why was this all his fault?

Kurt had known full well that the villa was in the '*campo*' or countryside, and that living on the site permanently was not allowed. He had paid the elderly farmer who owned the land a pittance for it as a result, and built the villa as a 'hospital job' to give workers he did not want to loose or make redundant something to do in a quiet period.

Using the in-house taxation team in Orlando's father's Madrid office he had off-set the costs of the building operation against tax and written off the cost of the building materials as 'wastage'.

It might have seemed a generous gesture to 'give' the villa to Orlando, but it was actually a carefully thought out tax dodge, and while Kurt tried to blame the architect, who was now backing away from his flailing arms and increasingly loud rants for not telling him it was illegal to build here, Orlando found his hackles begin to rise.

The young architect was not particularly pretty and was rather short, but in Orlando's mind she was still a female, and should be afforded at least some respect.

As Kurt's rant became rather personal about her appearance and called into question her qualifications, he could bear it no more, and at last he spoke.

What he said was certainly chivalrous initially, but ill-conceived given the situation they found themselves in, and if Orlando had managed to stop himself after the first couple of sentences it might have been all right. But his blood was up, and after the drubbing he had received from his father he was feeling far too angry and, in his view, unjustifiably hectored to stop now.

In the hearing of the now snivelling architect and the still cowering Town Hall official, he became expansive on Kurt's bullying and disregard for the local planning rules, his avoidance of national and local taxes and his arrogant attitude to blithely building in the '*campo*' and then handing the house over without warning them that it was illegally built.

And he didn't stop there. As Kurt swelled and clenched

and unclenched his ham-like fists at his side, Orlando added that he objected strongly to the way he leered at his fiancée, Ingrid, and made reference to certain infidelities Kurt had perpetrated with members of his father's staff in the recent past.

It was enough.

Kurt turned on his heel, slammed the door of his Bentley and drove hell-for-leather up the remains of the little track to the main road, where he grabbed his mobile phone, pressed two 'speed-dial' buttons and told Orlando's father that their business relationship was at an end.

-oooOoo-

Bobbie, when she turned on the waterworks, was one of those girls who everyone wanted to comfort, pat her little hand, say, "There, there", and tell her it would be all right.
But with nobody there to see her dissolve into tears now, she was on her own.

Although it was many years since Matravers Hall sat in its own grounds and the pampered owners just had to press a button to summon staff to help them with life's little problems, such as refilling the soda syphon or closing the blinds, the rooms and particularly the 'suites', in the section of the main part of the house that now comprised Bobbie's mother's 'wing', were still commodious and comfortable and always very, very quiet.

That quietness was now Bobbie's enemy.

If she had lived in a more modern house, such as 2 Easton Drive, the home of Janet and her Uncle Geoff, her crying would no doubt be heard by the other residents and a concerned voice would soon be heard enquiring if she was all right outside the door. But Matravers Hall was stoutly built and designed so that the privacy of an occupant could be guaranteed just by closing one of the tall and very thick oak doors.

The only other occupant of the house at the time was her mother, who was closeted in her office on the ground floor, and some distance from the Blue Room, the suite where Bobbie spent her time. Unless Bobbie opened the door, threw back her head and really bellowed, that industrious woman was unlikely to hear her, especially as she had the habit of turning off her hearing aid when she was working.

So Bobbie, in her misery, sat at the elegant, antique roll-top desk where she had been writing, or trying to write, and sobbed alone.

Until, that is, her mobile phone rang and the screen showed that her Uncle Geoff was calling.

-ooOoo-

Hospitals all have that chilly rubber-floored impersonality about them wherever you go.

The staff and management at the maternity suite

where Rosalind found herself now had tried their best to brighten the surroundings with jolly pictures of teddy-bears' picnics, and peaceful calming wall murals depicting mountain streams flowing through sunlit highlands, but there was no disguising the purposeful nature of the busy unit.

Things beeped and hissed, curtains rustled, nurses, midwives, daunted-looking fathers and hospital orderlies came and went, and nobody took any notice of Rosalind as she sat uncomfortably in the hygienic vinyl-covered armchair beside the metal-framed bed she had been allocated.

Rosalind was very bored.
It had been three hours since anything had actually happened and Mike and her mother had dashed home to get something to eat.

Helen said she would come back later if she could, but Rosalind knew she had to work, so that would not be for a while.

As a general rule, friends were not allowed in the maternity suite, so Rosalind and Helen perpetrated a small white lie and claimed they were sisters. Their appearance was so different that the Staff Nurse was obviously unconvinced, but, with a flicker of a smile, she had let it go and Helen had been allowed in. But that was ages ago, and with nothing happening there had been talk of sending Rosalind home.

Just as she was thinking that perhaps going home to

be in her own house with Mike and her mother might be a good idea, it started again.

That strange and unfamiliar wave, not of pain so much, but of a primeval certainty that something was about to happen.

-oooOoo-

Carlos and Maria had been dating on and off for about a year and, as her office was close to the Town Hall, Carlos had offered Maria a lift to the meeting at the remote villa.

Maria was unusual in that, as a fully qualified architect in a very male-dominated profession, she had not moved to Madrid or some other big city, where being a female in a 'man's profession' was not regarded as so uncommon.

Partly that was because the right opportunity had not presented itself yet, and partly it was because she was becoming very fond of Carlos.

He also had qualifications but she wished he had more self-assurance and tried a little harder to push himself forward. He could, she felt sure, easily get a job in Madrid in Local Government doing the same as he did now. It would pay much better and, if he would only do it, perhaps they could have a future together. But his shyness, whilst very attractive in one sense, and his gentle diffidence held him back.

Now that the enormous German builder had stormed

off, and the meeting seemed to be at an end, Maria blew her nose and Carlos opened the door of his car for her to get in.

The owner of the villa had ignored them after the shouting stopped and had now gone inside, so, after a moment of indecision, Carlos suggested they should go too.

'I'm sorry that big bully upset you, Maria,' Carlos offered as he closed his door.

Maria had wanted to remain professional, although she had never been spoken to like that before, and now that it was just her and Carlos in the car she slumped in her seat.

'Oh, Carlos!' she cried, falling into his arms. 'That horrible, horrible brute! I shall probably lose my job now if he tells my boss,' and the tears she had been trying so hard to hold back fell freely.

-ooOoo-

'Now when you come tomorrow...' Geoff started to say, but quickly realised that there was something wrong.

Bobbie's sniffs and the catch in her voice told him all he needed to know.

'Oh, Uncle Geoff!' she wailed now. 'Whatever am I going to do? I can't seem to string two coherent sentences together and I just can't decide what to write. And I really must reply to Rosy's letter!'

'Well, why don't you leave it until you come over tomorrow and, if you feel like it, we can sit down and have a crack at it together when you have done your unpacking.'

'Will it be just you and me?' sniffed Bobbie.

'Yes, just us. Janet will be at work, so it will be just like it used to be when I helped you with your homework.'

''Oh, Uncle Geoff,' there was a pause while Bobbie blew her nose, 'you always knew just what to do when I got upset and needed help. Just you saying that has made me feel a bit better already. Thank you.'

'No problem. I'm sure we will sort it out. Now then, when you come down, don't try to pack too many clothes and so on. There is not that much room in your little sports car and you don't want to overload it. And no doubt you will be going back home or off to a place of your own after a few days anyway....'

-ooOoo-

## Chapter 9

It was the hands that did it.

After all the stress, and then the relief that everything was all right, those perfect tiny hands finally made Mike cry.

She was so unbelievably beautiful. So perfect, and so tiny. His daughter, as the nurse gently took her back from him, had smiled, he was sure of it.

'Oh, now, don't get upset, Daddy, you can have another cuddle in a little while,' the nurse chuckled.

'Oh, I'm sorry …' spluttered Mike, 'It's just that ….'

'Quite all right, lovely, it happens all the time. Don't be embarrassed. At least you didn't pass out. You would be surprised how many do!'

Rosalind looked at her husband drying his tears. The rush of of love she felt now was all-embracing, and though she was smiling and laughing, she found that she was crying too.

-oo0Ooo-

Orlando did not feel like crying, but he did feel terribly

ashamed.

He had made the biggest mistake of his life, and he knew it.

When his father called him to ask him to fly to Madrid so that they could discuss how the company was going to be impacted now that Kurt had withdrawn his business, the full implications of what he had done hit him.

At first, there had been shouting over mobile phones, of course. But when his father calmed down a sort of gloomy resignation settled over their communications.

For a week Orlando had hidden himself away in the villa with Ingrid and communicated only by email with his office, and only then when he had to.

Ingrid had found him sitting on the terrace staring out to sea in the middle of the night on more than one occasion, but on the night it rained she found him still sitting there getting soaked. She told him she was concerned that he might be having some sort of a breakdown.

He assured her once again that he was all right as she drove him to the airport, but he knew that he wasn't.

-ooOOoo-

Ingrid woke with a start.

There was a large truck coming up the remains of the

little track, picking its way carefully towards the villa.

She grabbed her clothes and rapidly put them back on, and in her haste as she fought her way into the skimpy garments, she accidentally knocked over the water bottle she had put under her sun bed.

As the water spread over the terrace and dripped over the edge, she noticed that two cars were following the truck, and one of them was unmistakably a Police car!

Abandoning the struggle with her sun-dress, she grabbed her mobile phone and started dialling.

-ooo0oo-

The taxi that picked Orlando up from the airport and dropped him at the office was not from the usual company.

Orlando was surprised and dismayed when he found that he could not put the fare on the Company account and sign for it as he normally did, but that he had to pay the driver, in cash, when they arrived.

Even the concierge at the door seems frosty as he pressed the button to call a lift to take Orlando to the fifth floor, where his father waited, and as the doors slid open, a cold chill ran down Orlando's back that had nothing to do with the efficient air conditioning.

His father's secretary was on the phone and just waved him through to the inner office, but the customary welcoming smile was absent on her usually cheerful face.

Orlando took a seat in the little vestibule outside his father's office and waited until the muted sounds of his telephone conversation died away, before knocking on the door.

-oo0Ooo-

'Now, let's see,' said Geoff, 'I think we are getting somewhere, don't you, Bobbie?'

'As usual, Uncle Geoff, you have weaved your magic and rescued a poor beleaguered innocent young girl from the terrors she faced. Your exquisite resource, kind direction and endless patience have restored me from a gibbering wreck to the poised and confident person you see before you now. Where it not for your gentle expertise, the pressure on a delicate …'

'Yes, yes. Thats quite enough of that, thank you. I'm glad to see that you have regained your usual ability to talk absolute nonsense, but there is a limit, young Bobbie!' Geoff smiled broadly, 'Now how about we print this off and pop up to the Post Office to buy a stamp and post it. I'll even let you buy me an ice cream to say thank you.'

When Bobbie frowned at this idea, Geoff added, 'And I'll lend you the money to pay for it as well!'

-oo0Ooo-

# Chapter 10

As Ingrid packed her rucksack, the dust and noise was reaching a crescendo.

To give her time, the workmen had agreed to start the demolition on the wide two-storey wing that spread out from the main house and led away from the pool. With her bedroom in the single-storey wing at the opposite end of the building she had a small window of time to pack, call a taxi, and write two emails, one to her father and one to Orlando.

She had not sent the emails yet. That could wait. But the urgency she felt to get right away from the villa was increased as, glancing out of the floor-to-ceiling tinted glass windows, she saw a wall of masonry topple onto the marble-tiled terrace and crash into her beloved infinity pool. Around a quarter of the main structure of the villa succumbed to another blow from the enormous machine the truck had disgorged, which swung a brutal-looking concrete ball in an arc into the building.

Although the spectacle was slightly terrifying, she had come to terms with what her destiny held now.

She had broken her back-packing adventure around the world to take a job in a hotel and restore her finances, during which time Orlando and the chance to use her skills as an interpreter had cropped up. Whilst none of that was planned of course, she had been happy to settle for a while.

In the light of events now, however, her wanderlust was back with renewed vigour and she knew it was time to move on.

As the taxi, unable or unwilling to tackle the rough and damaged drive, stopped where the road ended, Ingrid laced up her walking boots, pulled her huge rucksack into place on her slender shoulders and turned her back on the villa for ever.

-ooOoo-

Paternity leave was a marvellous innovation and Mike intended to take full advantage of the time allotted to him to stay at home with Rosalind and his wonderful, exquisite, unbelievable little daughter, Jasmine.

They had chosen names months ago and, although Jasmine was on the long list, if it turned out to be a girl, it was not until the baby was born, and the moment that Mike and Rosalind looked at each other in the maternity unit and simultaneously said 'Jasmine' that the name cropped up again. And that was it.

The hospital cleaner packed away her materials, with

a satisfied smile. They included the jasmine-perfumed anti-bacterial air freshener she paid for herself and always used in an attempt to cheer up the maternity suite. The subtle smell of jasmine was her favourite.

-oo0Ooo-

Janet, letting herself into the house, was surprised to find nobody home.

Bobbie's little sports car was on the drive but Geoff's Jaguar had gone and she wondered what the pair of them were up to.

The day after tomorrow Bobbie was due to start work at XBS radio as an 'Advertising Sales Executive', or something like that. She hoped it was going to be a success and worried about Geoff and his concern that Bobbie would want to stay living at 2 Easton Drive for some time, and move with them wherever they moved to, when they finally found a house.

Poor Geoff. He was even jealous of the pot plants it seemed, and he did not want Bobbie disrupting the cosy routine they had developed over the months since he first moved in. It was sweet really, but he worried completely unnecessarily.

Janet had been in love just once before, with her maths teacher at her secondary school, when she was fourteen.
OK, it wasn't really love, she knew that now, but she thought it was at the time, and when the teacher left to go to another school she was heartbroken.

It was that innocent crush that decided Janet's career path. Mourning for what she thought was lost love, she made a conscious decision to ignore all distractions and throw herself into her studies.
As a result she was soon winning prizes and secured a scholarship as soon as her exceptional 'A' level results were published.

For seven long years Janet continued to ignore all external influences and studied hard. Instead of enjoying the usual distractions of youth, she focused ever harder on her academic career and was soon offered a rewarding position with a quite prestigious dental research company.

That led, in due course, to Janet having the ability and qualifications to practise hands-on dentistry which she had decided was what she really wanted to do and so she started applying for jobs.

But there was a problem.

Since her very earliest childhood Janet had sucked her thumb. The habit gave her comfort when the maths teacher moved to another school and then later she found sucking her thumb helped her to concentrate when she was studying.
It also gradually pushed her front teeth forward, and the problem was compounded when an accident on her bicycle forced her jaw out of alignment. After that, her twisted buck-toothed smile was not the best advert for any sort of dentistry.

The brace she wore at school was soon discarded so that the comforting and ever persistent thumb-sucking could continue and, despite her mother's best efforts, Janet's snaggled teeth just got gradually worse.

Several interviews for 'hands-on' dentistry positions produced no offers, although Janet was, by this stage, highly qualified and having collaborated on several research papers, had built a reputation in the theoretical side of her craft.

It was only when a softly spoken Sri Lankan dentist had the courage to explain the problem to her that the penny dropped. Dentists in private practice had to look like an advert for perfect dentistry, and however good they were at their jobs, the customers were not going to be put at their ease by a dentist with imperfect teeth.

There were tears at that interview, but the Sri Lankan knew a good thing when he saw it and he offered Janet what turned out to be the ideal opportunity.

Although she was massively over-qualified for the role, he offered her a job as a dental technician, working on creating, adjusting and manufacturing false teeth in the back room of his practice on just the basic salary the job commanded.

He explained that, if she was interested, in return he would initiate a twelve month programme to give Janet a smile of such devastating brilliance that she would be the best advertisement for his skills he could devise, and together they would write an authoritative paper for the British Dental Association on how it was done.

It was slow, painful, and for the Sri Lankan, very taxing work. Janet had to endure months of pain and weeks when she had to take sustenance through a straw as her teeth were removed, her jaw, which had to be broken, was rebuilt and her face was bruised and battered.

Then there was plastic surgery to hide the damage, and finally the installation of the enhanced perfect teeth she had now.

When it was all over, some months later, the Sri Lankan offered her a new deal. He would take her on as a full time practising dentist on full pay so long as she promised to stay with the practice for two years and allow herself to be photographed to demonstrate the capabilities of his practice.

Seventeen years later, long after the old Sri Lankan had retired, she was still with the same organisation and, now a full partner in the practice where she worked, she was doing rather well. The paper they wrote together is still one of the definitive works on radical dental reconstruction and regularly referred to in the university where Janet studied.

Geoff, of course, knew none of this and found it difficult to accept that such a radiantly lovely woman as Janet even gave him the time of day.

He adored Janet and she fell for his gentle, unassuming charm almost as soon as they met.

Now, as she heard his car pull into the drive, she found herself checking her hair in the hall mirror, running her tongue over her spectacularly enhanced teeth, and adjusting her clothing so that she looked her best.

-oo0Ooo-

Orlando opened Ingrid's email three hours after leaving his father's office.
By that time he was moderately drunk and well on the way to being very drunk indeed.

He suspected he knew what the contents of the message would be anyway, but he was surprised to learn that the demolition the villa was taking place already.

Orlando's time flitting between London, Madrid and the Costa Blanca was over now.

His father called the 'Human Resources Director' into the office and together they presented him with a settlement which, substantial though it was, would not last Orlando for long.

With Ingrid gone there seemed nothing to attract him back to the Costa Blanca now, and the little bit of furniture and clothing they arranged to have stored, before the inevitability of the demolition of the villa became a reality, had no real value. Orlando realised with a sigh that he had nowhere to put it anyway now and with no job, no salary, no home and no girlfriend, Spain as a whole held little attraction for him. Even his leased company cars in Spain and London had been confiscated and his life was changing completely.

He had checked into a hotel when he arrived, but he quickly cancelled his reservation when he realised that his father's company would not pay for the rather lavish suite he had reserved, and he knew that he would have to find somewhere much cheaper to stay tonight.

He sprinkled coins on the table of the bar and made his way rather unsteadily to the newsagents over the road. There he studied the local telephone directory that the proprietor lent him and called the number of a small hotel just round the corner.
If it was cash in advance, he was told, then yes they had a room for the night and he arranged to book it, giving his father's office address, as he realised he now had no other.

Next he found a cash-point and withdrew rather more cash than was necessary, walked round to the down-at-heel hotel, paid for his room and then retired to the scruffy bar downstairs to complete his efforts to get very drunk indeed.

-oo0Ooo-

## Chapter 11

Mike had to admit, even if only to himself, that he was pleased to be back at his desk.

Jasmine didn't seem to want to sleep at the appropriate time and slept like a pretty little princess when it was time for a feed.

And then there were the nappies.

With a sigh he turned his attention to his work. He noticed that his inbox was quite full, but he had expected that, and he rapidly sifted quite a portion of it into the bin. Other than the stuff on his computer, there was also a large brown envelope on his desk which he opened with some interest.

These were the details of the investigation into that international legal firm he had dealt with when they set up their London operation. He was intrigued to see what could possibly have gone wrong with such a straight-forward case.

The first page was one of those internal memos on green paper from his boss. It made for interesting reading, but did not clear up what the problem seemed to be.

The background, however, in the rest of the file, was that the Spanish Tax Office had opened an investigation which involved the Spanish equivalent of the Law Society, who oversaw the activities of lawyers in Spain. That related back, by a long list of coincidences, to some insignificant Town Hall in the Costa Blanca where a faceless Council Official had uncovered some irregular arrangements with a German builder.

It wouldn't have been anything that would normally have interested Mike's department except for the fact that the German builder mentioned had been instrumental as an investor in the lawyer's expansion outside Spain. Now certain tax irregularities, and the usual slightly dubious activities those people in the property world got up to with regards to where the money came from, had been exposed, and the usually sound fabric lawyers built their businesses on was coming apart in this case.

The Spanish tax office was interested in what could amount to 'money laundering' and got their British equivalents excited to make sure that the 'seed corn funds' which Mike's department administered for the Treasury to tempt businesses to invest in the UK had been appropriately dealt with. When British tax payers' money was involved, the level of scrutiny spending Departments like Mike's were subjected to was always intense, and the Treasury jealously guarded their turf where joint ventures with foreign investors were involved.

Mike read the file through with growing interest.

-ooOoo-

'Yays. I am a furry surprised too!'

Pedro, on Facetime, on Bobbie's iPad, had much to report.

'She justa came in the hotel to say the goodbye. She come for the Victor to say she going, not stay with the Orlando no more. Thats a when she telling the villa been … how you say? … admonished?'

'Demolished! Do you mean demolished, as in knocked down?' said Bobbie, amazed.

'Yays. Ees furry big surprising! The Orlando villa he out in the campo where is no allowed build the flash places. When the a Town Hall see thees they furry cross and bring it down!'

'So Ingrid and Orlando couldn't live there anymore?' Bobbie could hardly believe what she was hearing.

'No. Yays. So when the Orlando he go Madrid, the Ingrid she off out of it right quickie. They finish. She go back the Sweden see the papa of she.'

Pedro paused to collect his thoughts now. He needed to make sure he was not misunderstood. He did not want Bobbie to think Ingrid had come to the hotel to see him.

'Bobbie, I no say she coming see me. She coming see the Victor. She know he hang about in a the hotel all the day. I furry surprise see her, but I furry glad she no come see for me only. I only got the hots for you Bobbie, no want see the Ingrid no more!'

'Oh, Pedro, you are so sweet!' exclaimed Bobbie.

-ooOOoo-

Carlos hoped things had not got out of control.

It had taken all his courage to ask to see the Mayor and his boss and explain what he had heard at the villa and the content of the row between the German builder, Maria the architect, and that nasty lawyer.

He was glad he had done it, though. Nobody should be allowed to speak to his Maria like that, and if she was to get into trouble with her boss, he wanted to do all he could to help her.

His Maria? He caught himself.

Was she his Maria?

Now that he came to think about it, he really hoped she was.

Perhaps, if she had to leave the architect she worked for and move to Madrid to get another job, he could, maybe he should, look for a job there too.

His Maria?

Carlos wondered if she felt the same way about him. If he had to move to Madrid to stand by her side, he would be proud to do it.

Yes, proud.

He reached for his mobile phone and dialled her number.

-ooo0oo-

'The morning one, the DJ, I mean, is a pop-eyed, ageing, adenoidal anachronism, who could do with a more age-appropriate haircut and thinks he is rather a wow with the ladies.'

Bobbie was amusing her audience with a word picture of the staff at XBS Radio after her first week in her new job there.

'There is this room with grey foam rubber on the walls which they call the studio suite, where they broadcast from. Lionel, the lecherous librarian lurks there, sorting out the tunes they play on his computer and answering banal questions, like why such and such a band moved from this record label to another in 1976. I mean, who actually cares?'

'So it's not very high-brow, then?' asked Janet.

'Well, not in the morning, or when the music shows are on anyway. It gets a bit more interesting in the afternoon when they have a chat show and a news round-up. But it is all mass-market stuff, really. Pretty forgettable, to be honest.'

'But what about the selling the advertising bit? How is that going?' asked Geoff.

'Ah, now there you take me into deep waters. I'm not actually sure how that all works quite yet. I've been round a couple of times with Lindsay to be introduced to some of the clients, but it all seems to involve sitting about having coffees in cafes or sometimes lunch in little bistros talking about anything but advertising. Lindsay seems to just pop round to see the same list of people on a sort of rota, and that's it.'

'Good heavens,' said Geoff, who had a very different idea of what selling jobs involved.

'We have sales meetings on a Monday, I'm told, but I haven't been to one of those yet, so I'm not sure what to expect.' Bobbie picked at her side-salad. 'I would have thought Rosy would be here by now. Do you suppose she is not coming?'

The plan had come together very quickly following Rosy's positive reaction to Bobbie's letter. They had decided to meet on neutral territory in the steakhouse near the station. Janet and Geoff had been invited along for moral support and also, no doubt, to pay the bill after the meal they planned to have there.

They had arrived a little early as Bobbie, who would never admit that she was nervous, hurried them out of the house. So, to fill the time and for something to do, they had chosen a table and helped themselves from the salad cart, and they now sat watching the entrance and moving the wilting salad around their bowls.

'I'm sure she will be here in a minute or two,' said Janet encouragingly, and at that moment the door to the street opened and in walked Rosy.

-ooOOoo-

Geoff recognised Edmund straight away.

The gormless, pimply youth who had been dispatched to collect Rosy's clothes in his tiny hatchback all those months ago was following her into the steak-house now.
Rosy, usually boisterous, full of bonhomie and loud, was subdued. Shy even, and she stood uncomfortably by the door.

Bobbie got up and went to meet her.

'Want some more salad, Janet?' said Geoff, pushing back his chair and starting to move towards the salad cart.

'Oh, no, Geoff,' said Janet sternly. 'You sit down and wait. Bobbie might need our help at any moment.'

Geoff did as he was told, although a quiet sneak to the other end of the restaurant seemed to him to be far preferable than watching the fireworks at close quarters.

'Hi,' said Bobbie uncertainly.

'Hi,' replied Rosy, and that about exhausted the opportunities for conversation for the moment until, with a cough, Edmund spoke.

'Er, yes, well,' he began, though not confidently, 'Hullo again, Bobbie, old thing. Hope you don't mind but Rosy needed a lift over …' and then he stood awkwardly shuffling his feet and opening and closing his mouth like a goldfish.
As this small talk rapidly ran down, Geoff decided to intervene.

On his feet now he grabbed Edmund's limp arm and shook the hand on the end of it heartily.

'Hello there, Edmund. How nice to see you again. We have a table just over there. Perhaps you would like to join us?'

Edmund, though somewhat startled to have been grasped so confidently, now had clear stage directions to follow, and he quickly caught on to what was expected of him.

'What? Eh? Yes. I mean, rather. Jolly decent of you and all that sort of thing,' and like a lamb he followed Geoff to the table to be introduced to Janet.

Bobbie was eyeing Rosy while this little exchange took place.

Her face was puffy. Had she been crying?

'Thanks for inviting me,' she said huskily, 'I hope you don't mind my brother coming along, I just needed ….'

'Not at all,' said Bobbie, taking her lead, 'I hope you can excuse Geoff and Janet joining us, I rather thought …'

The conversation then stalled again until Janet bounced up and greeted Rosy with seemingly unforced ease and invited her to join the others at the table.

Geoff, Bobbie noticed, was heading for the salad cart.

-oooOoo-

Edmund found the situation excruciatingly embarrassing, of course. He was essentially a passive soul and he hated difficult situations.

However much he would have liked the ground to open up and swallow him, he had to accept that it was unlikely and so, studiously avoiding eye contact with his sister, he made a play of eating his bread roll in the hope that nobody would talk to him, or expect him to speak.

He recalled now the privations he had already experienced today.

Having been unceremoniously marched to his car when he tried to get out of taking Rosy on this trip, he was cornered.

He was always rather terrified of his sister as they

grew up and he dreaded the school holidays when they were all at home. Usually Rosy and their elder brother seemed to take it in turns to order him about.

Now with university as his refuge, he did manage to avoid most situations involving his siblings, but there were still holidays and there were two solid weeks left of the present one until he could go back to the relative tranquility of his studies.

Edmund had just managed to scrape into a red-brick university in Reading, Berkshire, to study Estate Management and he was not finding it particularly easy. The hope was that he would eventually be employed in some role in the management of the family farms and estates which would, according to his father, not be too taxing.

He knew that he was not clever, and certainly could not rise to the intellectual heights his sister seemed to conquer with such ease. As the second son of an old established family his choices were somewhat limited. He would have to earn a living and could not depend on an income from the extensive landholdings his brother would inherit, but he was unfitted for the cut and thrust of commerce and was too timid to face life in the pulpit, as his mother would have preferred.

A life in the Church was not for him and he was not in the least bit religious, being unable to grasp what all the fuss was about. Apart from an enforced period as a choirboy, he generally avoided churches and clergymen, in particular, at all costs.

He did, however, have some sporting blood and loved to join his former public school friends at the horse races. He would have liked to have been on his way to the evening meeting at Epsom, where he had received a solid tip on a certain horse and deposited a sizeable proportion of his meagre wealth at the local bookmakers on its nose earlier in the day.

As he chewed disconsolately on the dry bread and tried not to look at his sister across the table now, he remembered his telephone conversation this morning. Simon 'Stinker' Stannard had been quite certain about the horse.

'I'd say Bananarama can't fail against that field, even if it stops for a bracing nosebag halfway round! This one is a flier!'
As this came from a usually reliable source Edmund was impressed. But there was more.
'We are all going in big on this one as a sort of starter to the evening's jollity. If you will come in with us and all goes well, we should get on at a good price and be set fair for a punt on Bluebottle in the next race.'

'All right, Stinker, I'm in!' Edmund had said, 'I've also heard that Bluebottle is much favoured in the second race. The bookies know that too, of course, so the on-course odds might not be too attractive, but they might improve once we get there. If we go in with enough winnings from the first race we should be well set, and then it's but a short step to invest modestly in

Connolly's Lass in the next on the card, and there we make our killing.'

'Quite,' Stinker said. 'So you will toddle round to your local turf accountant and put the consortium's money on as agreed then, Ed, old chap? I'd go myself but the Guv'nor has got me tied down helping the stable girls clean out the old horse box ready for the big point-to-point meet at the weekend.'

'Consider it done, Stinker, old man!' Edmund had replied.

He was wrenched back from his reverie by the chap sitting on his left at the table in the steak-house.

Geoff, was it? Yes, that was his name, and he was asking Edmund if he would like a side-salad.

-ooOoo-

Mike had to drag himself to work.

Until now he had no idea a newborn baby could create such an upheaval. They had had very little sleep and Rosalind was becoming fractious and argumentative. In some ways the prospect of the relative calm of the office and even his busy desk was a comfort. At least it was better than fitfully dozing off on the train.

Waiting for him today was an internal memo about the odd case of the Spanish lawyers. It began with a translated statement from the Spanish Tax Authorities to the effect that the German builder involved in financing the lawyer's expansion had been arrested on suspicion of fraud.

Although there was no further detail on that point, the implication for Mike's department was all too clear. There would now be a root and branch investigation by the Treasury into the processes they followed and the negotiations they held.

Mike groaned. He knew that his office had handled the situation entirely correctly and nothing untoward would be found as far as they were concerned. His own limited involvement was properly documented, but these investigations took time and resources, put everyone on edge, and slowed all the other work down.

He picked up the memo and went to see his boss.

-ooo0oo-

Rosy sat uncomfortably on the edge of her chair.

She was not at all sure that she would be able to eat anything, and although Bobbie's letter had gone some way to offering her reassurance, now that they were face-to-face, she still felt distinctly ill-at-ease.
Janet was doing her best to jolly everyone along, although even she was not immune to the awkward atmosphere. But it was Geoff who opened the debate.

'Right,' he said, returning from the salad cart with a hastily-collated collection of fresh items, 'I think we need to clear the air and you two need to take stock of what has gone on. Here are the keys of the Jaguar, Bobbie. You and Rosy go and sit in the car for a few minutes and say what you need to each other without an audience. I will come out and get you in ten minutes time and then, hopefully, we can get something more substantial to eat than just this ruddy salad.'

It was a sound suggestion and both girls smiled in relief.

When they had gone Janet congratulated Geoff on his idea and they settled down to toy with the salad once more.

-oo0oo-

Bobbie, in the driver's seat, waited for Rosy to settle on the passenger side of the car.

'Good old Uncle Geoff,' she said. 'Trust him to come up with a way to break the tension.'

'Did I detect his touch in your lovely letter?' Rosy asked.

'Well, yes. I hope you don't mind, but he has always been my knight in shining armour and since my father died has sort of taken over the role of parent as well as mentor and friend.'

'I confess I had mummy's help to write to you when I did.' Rosy admitted. 'She is a Doctor of Philosophy and despite that she always seems to know the right thing to say.'

'We could have done with them alongside us in Spain,' said Bobbie.

'You are right, Bobbie. Then we might not have made such an awful hash of things …' A little sniff escaped Rosy and she felt in her pocket for her handkerchief. 'I really am most awfully sorry, you know …'

'Oh, Rosy, I do know. And I'm terribly sorry too. Can't we just put it all behind us and go back to how we were?' It was Bobbie's turn to reach for a tissue from the door pocket in her uncle's car.

'There is quite a bit you don't know that perhaps I ought to tell you before you make your mind up though, Bobbie,' Rosy admitted.

'And a lot has happened since then. I found out the other day that Orlando and Ingrid have split up and their villa has been demolished!' Bobbie said.

'Demolished? … Well, I'm surprised it has gone that far already.'

'I'm sorry, what do you mean?'

'Well, perhaps I had better start from the beginning.' Rosy made herself more comfortable on the leather seat.

'The beginning?' Bobbie was confused.

'You remember, in my letter, I explained that I had

walked out of the villa? Well, I had to walk about three solid miles to the nearest little town, in tight shoes and on a hot day too.' Rosy watched Bobbie's face carefully as she proceeded, this was probably all news to her. 'When I got there I found the little Town Hall and made myself known to the people there. I explained about being at the villa and Orlando's beastly ideas to involve me in embezzlement. The receptionist there, who spoke really good English, by the way, insisted that I should speak to some officials, and when I'd done that, with her translating, they asked if I wanted them to get a policeman so that I could make something they called a "*denuncia*", a bit like a statement, accusing Orlando of kidnapping me.'

'Good heavens!' exclaimed Bobbie.

'Indeed, and that is not the half of it. They asked me to explain where I had been and with the help of the English-speaking lady and a map, I showed them where I had walked from. At first they said that I was mistaken because that area was just what they called the "*campo,*" or countryside, and there were no houses there, but I showed them the pictures on my phone that we took of the infinity pool and the terraces and the magnificent view, when we first went there. That is when they went to get the Mayor and some other officials and made me tell the story all over again.'

Rosy blew her nose and continued.

'They seemed very interested in the villa and the English-speaking lady explained to me that they had not been aware that it had been built, and that it was illegal to build in that area.'

'But how did you get home?' asked Bobbie.

'Well, the lady, the English-speaking one, was an absolute angel and she arranged for me to talk to a travel agent who booked me a flight the next day. And then she fixed me up with a room in the most delightful little *hostal* … not a bit like Youth Hostels in this country, really much more of a boutique hotel … and she even arranged for them to have a taxi pick me up and take me to the airport in the morning.'

Bobbie was suddenly aware that she was staring at Rosy with her mouth open and, as she adjusted her facial muscles, she jumped six inches as Geoff knocked gently on the car window.

-ooOoo-

By the time they had reached the desserts and Bobbie had told the story of letting all the water out of Orlando's pool with Pedro, the atmosphere was quite festive.

Edmund had enjoyed the story about the pool and chortled happily, and even Geoff, who had initially disapproved strongly, found himself laughing out loud at Bobbie's unique way of telling the tale.

Rosy and Bobbie sat next to each other, and in spite of her earlier misgivings, Rosy had now found her appetite and tucked into a substantial steak with all the trimmings and a large portion of cheesecake.

The two girls laughed and reminded each other of incidents from their university days with which to entertain the rest of the table.

It seemed everything was going well, and until his mobile phone buzzed with a text message, even Edmund was enjoying himself.

Bluebottle, the most likely choice in the second race on the card at the evening meeting at Epsom, had won easily, but Edmund's confidence in Bananarama, the consortium's horse for the first race, was mis-placed. That horse came a distant sixth so the investment they planned for Bluebottle evaporated before it could be put into the bookmaker's hands. Edmund, anxious to play up to the standards of the rest of the consortium, had rather over-extended himself and the amount he had lost would make a serious dent in his always precarious finances, which would be felt for some time.

-ooOoo-

# Chapter 12

The search for property had all but stalled.

Whilst Janet had a buyer for 2 Easton Drive at a good price, there was a chain of sales involved and somewhere along the line there was a problem.
The 'first time buyer' at the bottom of the pile was experiencing difficulties with his mortgage, and while he tried to sort it out, the property he wanted to buy had been put back on the market.

The timing of these things is never ideal, but now they had a solution.

In the couple of months since the buyer was found for 2 Easton Drive, Geoff's former marital home had been sold and legal completion was due in just a few days, so if they did find something they liked Geoff had explained that he could buy it with the money left over after his small mortgage was paid off. Geoff's ex-wife had secured another property and moved out, so the situation at that house at least was resolved.

Before his house was sold, Geoff and Janet had seen several houses they liked and had got as far as making an offer on one, but because they were what the agent called 'non-proceedable buyers' (whatever that meant) the offer was not accepted and the house was promptly sold to somebody else.

Today, however, Janet had received details of a rather pretty, detached Victorian house in one of the better roads that they knew they liked. It was not big, in fact it was probably the smallest house in the road, and the agent's exuberant description could not hide the fact that it was in need of some 'updating', but it had roses round the door, a 'cottage garden' and plenty of 'potential'.

Janet knew that there was little point in forwarding the email containing the details to Geoff, because he struggled with even basic mobile phone technology, so she rang him up.

Normally Janet was too busy to make phone calls from work, but when a patient was late for an appointment, she grabbed the chance to make the call.

Geoff was just finishing his washing the old Jaguar and had left his phone on the hall table to avoid it getting wet, but he managed to get to it just before the infernal thing diverted the call to some sort of answering service, that he could never seem to access.

He was surprised to hear from Janet and for a moment worried that something might be wrong. Duly reassured by her excited, breathless voice, he listened with rising interest to her description of the house.

They had driven down this particular road a few

times.

It was very close to where Janet's friend Lucy lived in a rather grand house on an exclusive private estate, and they liked the area. The other houses in the road were all detached four, and five bedroomed modern houses. Just five or six of the original properties, a mixture of semis and small villas built around the turn of the century, remained, and with the exception of this one, each of them had been substantially extended.

Geoff agreed that Janet should not hesitate to make an appointment to view the house, and as soon as she said goodbye to him, Janet called the agent.

The first available 'slot' for viewing was at nine in the morning on Saturday, and Geoff and Janet were sitting outside in the Jaguar when, at five minutes past, the agent arrived with the key.

As Ms. Susan Sanderson, from Stiffhams Estate Agents, introduced herself, Geoff could not help smiling. The poor woman had a pronounced lisp and had possibly accentuated the problem by referring to herself as 'Ms.' given that her name contained a series of buzzing sounds when she said it out loud.
But Geoff quickly tuned out her somewhat persistent buzzing summary as she opened the door of the little house and he was able to take in what was revealed.

The hallway, with its tiled floor and high ceilings, looked quite inviting. The original coving and ceiling roses were still in place and the polished wooden stair rail, with a curly newel post, looked original too.

The house was dated, certainly. It had probably last been decorated at least twenty-five years previously, but it was clean and tidy and smelt slightly of polish.

There was a downstairs bathroom which was in dire need of replacement, and another upstairs, with a rather sudden pink suite that would definitely have to go.

Janet agreed with the agent that the small kitchen was also in need of a refit, but that opening it up with the dining room next door would make it into a very pleasant room, with french doors to the garden.

The two bedrooms were adequate rather than spacious, and there were signs of damp in one corner, but the house had not been occupied for some time, so the agent said, it might just be condensation.

The so called 'cottage garden' did rather push the credibility of even the most ebullient of agent's descriptions. It was just a small square of concrete with a long thin strip of jungle leading to a crumbling wall and a wonky metal and asbestos single garage at the rear, which was served by a little access lane.

The agent did not have the key to the garage but it was easy to see what was inside because the door at the rear had a substantial gap on one side where the crooked structure had dropped away from it. There was no doubt, Geoff thought, that one encouraging push would see the whole thing give up the struggle and collapse.

The house would need a lot of work, but it was lovely and sunny and in a great location, so when Janet slipped her hand into his and they exchanged glances, they both knew that this was the one.

-ooOOoo-

That evening Bobbie was to be found on her iPad, talking to Pedro on FaceTime in Spain.

'And Rosy has a potential job offer in London so will want to move nearer, to be able to commute, if she gets it. So we are thinking about looking for a flat or something to share.'

'Please what is "commute", Bobbie?' Pedro asked, and as she explained the concept, Janet handed her a cup of tea and treated her to one of her dazzling smiles.

'OK,' said Pedro, 'I seeing. Now I got the big thing a tell you, so please to listen careful.'

'Hi, Pedro!' chirruped Janet.

'Hola, Janet. *Que tal*? I mean how was it?'

'I'm fine thanks, and you?'

'I all good. Please but I a speak Bobbie now, is furry important.'

'Sorry, Pedro, I didn't mean to interrupt.'

'Is no problem, Janet. I no be rude, please excuse.'

Bobbie and Janet exchanged glances and, thinking

this might be private, Janet headed for the kitchen.

'So what was it you wanted to say?' asked Bobbie.

'Well, yays … Is no fix yet. He take a many weeks to fix, but if he do then is furry exciting. I full of, how you say? Constipation?'

'I think you mean "anticipation"!' laughed Bobbie.

'Yays, that's a it. Antipasta, like a you say.'

Bobbie let it go.

'As I am say, is no fix, but is furry good chance maybe, I hoping.'

'What is?' said Bobbie.

'Like what I telling, is furry exciting. I got the chance maybe get job in the Sabadell Bank in the England.'

'Pedro!' squeaked Bobbie, which made Janet rush back from the kitchen, 'You mean you could come to live in England?'

'Yays. Perhaps a maybe. If it can be fix. The Sabadell she looking for the students working to do the international bank based in the London.'

'Gosh! Really? Oh, Pedro, that is so exciting!'

'But please, Bobbie, no boil over yet. Is no fix. Is only chance. I got to go the interview and do the little exam. Only if is OK then the visit the college in the London fix up the course. Is much to learn then. Next the working in the bank some of the days too.'

'So will you move to England permanently?'

'Well is depends. I Spanish citizen be working abroad so I need first the student visa, then the permiso … the papers let me do the working in the London. Oh, Bobbie … is no fix but I furry excited!'

'Oh, Pedro, I'm very excited too! When will you know?'

'Is many step to take, they a saying. We have to go slow. It taking the time. But the interview, she on the, you say, Monday. If this pass me, it could happen, yes?'

'Brilliant!' Bobbie had picked up her iPad and was dancing round the room with it.

'So, Bobbie, I a have the furry important question. Please to stop the wiggling about, you make a me feel sick! Now please I furry much need know thees.'

Bobbie sat down on the sofa.

'Now I ask the big question you. I furry hoping this not go wrong …'

For a fleeting second Bobbie thought he might be going to propose.

'Is big move for me, if it fix. I need know, Bobbie, how you feeling. I … I need know if you want the Pedro hanging about in the England. If you like me not come, I stay Spain, then I … I understand. But … Oh, Bobbie ….'

'Pedro. Dear, sweet Pedro. I would love it if you came to live in England and we could see each other more. That would be really great.'

'This a you mean, Bobbie? You liking the Pedro being there? You think we can be ... how you say? ... Go steady ... be a couple, yays?'

'I think we have been a couple for a while now Pedro. There is nobody else I would rather be with.'

'Oh! Is same, same for me, Bobbie. I no looking the other girls. They look me, I no look them. Not since meet you. You the best, no question. I'm think you all the time and a miss you furry much!'

Janet had heard enough and retired once more to the kitchen. She had guessed what was coming next and Bobbie did not need an audience.

'Bobbie ... You really feel like this? Bobbie ... Bobbie ... I never feel this a way for any girl before ... Bobbie ... Oh, Bobbie. I'm think I'm love you!'

-ooo0oo-

Rosy was offered the job on the spot and, when they asked if she would take it, she said she without hesitation that she would.

Docket, Fawcett, Barrel PLC was a leading accountancy practice with an international reputation and many prestigious clients. They only took the brightest and the best, and for them, Rosy fitted the bill perfectly.

Now she had to find somewhere to live within an easy commute of their extensive London headquarters, where she would be working.

On the way back to the station, after the interview, she stopped to look in some of the estate agents windows and was horrified at the extortionate rents being charged for even the most modest places in the city, and it made it obvious that she must join the ranks of the commuters travelling in to work each day from some suburban location.

Now that she thought about it, Bobbie was right about it making sense for them to share a flat or something in the area where Geoff and Janet lived now. If they could find something economical enough for both of them, the commute was not too bad, and it would be great fun to live with the effervescent Bobbie, sharing digs as they had at university.

As she found a seat on the train, she took out her mobile phone and prepared to tell Bobbie the good news.

-oo0Ooo-

The world of local radio advertising was gradually being revealed to Bobbie and, as she attended her first sales meeting, the slightly more pressurised side of the business of selling was exposed.

The meeting was chaired by Ralph, a tall string bean of a man with horn-rimmed glasses and bony hands and fingers, which he used to express himself as he spoke and to drum on the table when he expected answers.

He asked Lindsay for her report and then kept interrupting her with quite aggressive questions about whether she had asked this or that and how she had promoted the new campaign they were running.

As Bobbie listened to this she realised that Lindsay's report was almost entirely a fabrication, and bore little relation to the chatty meetings she had been to with the various clients they had visited together. Bobbie was listening intently in these little meetings and she very much doubted if she would have missed the discussion Lindsay was describing in which she said they talked about new spending targets and increasing their exposure to radio advertising.

Being the new girl, of course, she did not feel she could say anything, but as soon as the meeting was over she asked Lindsay about it.

'Oh, you don't have to worry about Ralph,' she said. 'You can feed him any old tosh at those meetings and he goes away happy. He is supposed to visit all the clients himself, but he never does. He just likes to give the impression that he is in charge. He is the owner's nephew, you see.'

Bobbie didn't see at all, but Lindsay had more to say.

'No, the one to be worried about is Baldy Head, the M.D. He will tear you apart if he thinks you are slacking. But he likes written reports from Ralph and we only have to go to what he calls 'Management Meetings' once a quarter with him. Baldy ... his name is really Barney ... hates Ralph, but he can't sack him, what with him being the boss's nephew, so he gives him all sorts of hell at these meetings and that kinda takes the pressure off us.'

'But,' said Bobbie, 'if Ralph reports what you said and Bald ... I mean Mr Head ... finds out it isn't true; won't he start asking questions?'

'No, child. That is the beauty of it. Baldy is actually hoping Ralph feeds him a load of nonsense so that one day he can catch him out, tell his uncle what he is doing and then the old boy will chuck him out. But Ralph is clever. He creams off the big important customers and deals with them himself. He keeps them as his exclusive clients so whenever a big contract is landed it is always Ralph that lands it, and he makes sure his uncle knows all about it. All we have to do is keep the rest of the clients happy and we are in clover.'

'What about finding new customers and all that sort of thing?' Bobbie asked.

'Well, yes. We are supposed to find new clients, but that is really hard work and is only really possible if we have some new bargain offer to show them. Otherwise we generally don't even get through the door. So what we do is keep the existing advertisers sweet and let Ralph and Baldy worry about finding big new clients to impress his uncle.'

Bobbie was about to say 'But ...' when she noticed Lindsay was waving a coffee mug at her.

'Now be a love and fill this up while I make some phone calls. Two sugars.'

-oo0Ooo-

They offered the asking price straight away, and when Geoff explained that the sale of his house had 'exchanged contracts', the offer was accepted.

That evening as they sat close together on the sofa, looking at the agent's details, Janet raised the issue that had been concerning her.

'Geoff, I know the agent was happy when you explained about your house being sold, but mine isn't. The chain of sales is not complete so nothing can move until it is.'

'That's all right, Janet. My share of the money from the sale of the house is almost enough to buy it anyway and I do have some savings.'

'But we are supposed to be doing this together. Half each we agreed.'

'Yes, love, but we don't want to lose this one, do we, so let's worry about the financial details when we have got a sale tied up.'

Janet chewed her lip.

'But it's not just the buying it, is it. It needs a new

kitchen and the bathroom changing and all that sort of thing. How are we going to pay for that? Until I've sold 2 Easton Drive I'm not sure I've got enough money for all that. And until this place is sold I can't honour my half of the deal.'

Geoff looked at Janet's concerned face and decided it was time he told her about his conversation with his solicitor this morning. He had been saving it for a romantic dinner, but now seemed a good time to mention it.

'Janet,' he said now, taking both her hands in his, 'I heard from the solicitors this morning that the first part of the divorce has come through and we should get the papers by the end of next week.'

'Oh, Geoff…'

'So that means that I am about to be free of any marital constraints. In turn that means we can start talking in terms of joint ownership of everything we both have, so it won't matter who has put in what. That is, of course, if you would consider consenting to be my wife.'

'Geoff? I …'

And at that moment Bobbie's key turned in the front door and her cheery 'hello' made this precious moment dissolve with a pop.

She also had Rosy with her.

## BOBBIE AND THE SPANISH CHAP

-ooOoo-

## Chapter 13

Mike would inevitably miss his usual train now and the fourth meeting of the day about the Spanish law firm showed no sign of winding up soon.

He had sent Rosalind a text warning her that he would probably be late and her curt, one word reply spoke volumes.

The word "Right." when used with the correct intonation can be damningly sarcastic and even when written, in the appropriate context, can leave the reader in no doubt as to the sender's feelings.

Mike had tried his best to push things along, but these new external consultants the Treasury had appointed to run the process seemed to be in no hurry at all. It occurred to him that perhaps they were being paid by the hour so the longer it took the more of the Government's money they soaked up.

The self appointed 'chairman' of proceedings in this particular meeting was clearly past retirement age and announced that he was engaged by the external company on a 'consultancy basis'. The no-doubt bloated fee he would earn for his afternoon's work was justified by his experience in heading up fraud investigations with the Metropolitan Police where, he reminded the meeting on numerous occasions, he had spent a long and successful career.

He was clearly enjoying himself and certainly would not win any prizes for brevity. His expansive little interventions were causing everyone in the meeting to shuffle uncomfortably in their chairs and surreptitiously glance at their watches.

Something of a crescendo was reached, however, when the hawkish lawyer from the office of the British Law Society, the body which represented those employed in the legal profession, spoke up.

'It seems to me,' he stated, 'that it would be prudent to establish whether the partners, or are they directors, of the firm are all fully qualified to work in the United Kingdom. If not, they could simply be acting as managers and instructing British solicitors working under them, and in their employ, how to proceed. The fraud, if there is one, could be nothing to do with the legitimate practice of law and only to do with the bona fides of those who put in the finance to start and run the operation.'

Obviously this was designed to elevate the members of the Law Society above suspicion, but in the context of foreign investment, he had a point.

'Perhaps,' he continued, 'The representatives of the Trade Department could tell us what research was done into the background of the persons who set up this business, here and abroad, and by what measure they approved this investment and the setting up of this business in the UK.'

That was taking the process right back to square one. The 'chairman', doubtless seeing another fat fee on the horizon for more work, grabbed it with both hands.

'My dear fellow,' he said. 'You have absolutely grasped the issue at hand. So far we have only discussed the system used to encourage foreign investment, but we have not touched on the fine details of the due process and inducements individuals such as these are offered to invest in Great Britain by the various Government departments involved. Unpacking that will probably take us some considerable time.'

Mike groaned inwardly. This was precisely the area that had been extensively explored in the first two of todays' laborious meetings, and now the roundabout seemed to be going round again.

-oo0Ooo-

'So, the way I see it,' said Rosy, helping herself to another digestive biscuit, 'if we can find a reasonably priced flat or whatever, within walking distance of the station, we can have a jolly old time and both get to work quite easily.'

'That makes absolute sense to me,' said Geoff, who was quietly relieved that Bobbie's time living in 2

Easton Drive was soon to come to an end, 'And would you like me to help you to find this place?'

'Oh, would you, Uncle Geoff!' smiled Bobbie. 'With your being on the spot, as it were, and given your vast and very recent knowledge of the local property market, with all the contacts you must have built up, I'm sure you can soon unearth something.'

'Well, I can at least try,' said Geoff.

'We,' Bobbie offered, 'shall want something suitable for a couple of bright young girls about town, with two well-appointed bedrooms, a stylishly furnished reception room, kitchen and all the usual offices.'

'But mostly we will want something cheap!' interposed Rosy, smiling indulgently at Bobbie, 'I'm going to be earning good money, but not that good, and while Bobbie isn't getting any commission yet we will have to cut our coat according to our cloth.'

'Well, yes,' said Bobbie doubtfully. 'But we won't have to live in anything like those ghastly student flats we looked at in Cambridge will we? I don't think I could stand all that three-day-old curry and peeling posters on the walls.'

'Three-day-old curry on the walls?' chuckled Geoff.

'Oh, yes,' said Rosy. 'And worse. We saw places that would make your flesh crawl before we were lucky enough to grab a place in "Halls" on the campus.'

'I shall make a start in the morning,' said Geoff with a determined nod to each of them. Nobody, he thought, was going to make his little Bobbie live in a dump like that, even if he had to subsidise the rent a little until Bobbie started earning commission.

'Why not make a start now?' said Janet, and passing Geoff her iPad, pointed out adverts for places to rent locally that she had found while they were chatting.

-oo0Ooo-

By the time Rosy left they had a short list of three flats for Geoff to ring up about in the morning and while Bobbie went to her room to 'FaceTime' Pedro, Janet was anxious to speak.

'Geoff, before Rosy and Bobbie arrived you were talking about the house and …'

'And asking you to marry me. Yes, it all comes back to me now,' smiled Geoff.

'Well, look, there is something I have got to talk to you about first. I'm sorry Geoff but …'

Geoff felt his stomach tighten and he instinctively reached into his pocket for his indigestion tablets.

'Oh, Janet. What's the matter?'

Janet was crying.

-oo0Ooo-

'I got a you email about the flat with the Rosy. This sounds all furry good,' said Pedro. 'If you place near the a railway, is easy for me to come from the college see you, if the Sabadell they want the Pedro, no?'

'Stop teasing me, Pedro! Tell me how the interview went! I have been like a cat on a hot tin roof all day worrying about it!'

'Why you been on the tin roof? I no understand?'

'Pedro! Tell me about the interview!'

'All right, Bobbie, calm a down,' chuckled Pedro, 'I telling now. Is furry big office. I not finding the right place at first but a then a lady coming in she tell me she show me where to go and it turns out she is one of the people gonna interview me! This mean I get a little time talk her before the interview. She say me many things they looking for. I don think she meant to say this but maybe she like the Pedro and wanna help.'

'Well, that was lucky! What happened next?'

'Well, I got wait in the small room with the other persons ... how you say? Candle... Candy ...'

'Candidates. Get on with it! What happened?'

'Well I got do the tests all OK, no problema, top marks. Then I go see the interview and the lady she there smiling me.'

'So you passed the psychometric tests?'

'No. I just a pass the little tests they give. What means this cycle thing?'

'Sorry, that is what we call them in England. What happened in the interview.'

'Well, the nice lady she say me I pass the little tests good. Then the big man, top chap, he start the talking, in the English and the Spanish, see if I keep up. I got no problem, he talk simple. Then the fat lady she ask me all about my a family and if I no like a being away, maybe miss them. I say yes I will, but I told them about you, Bobbie, then they all looking each other smiling.'

'I'm not sure I would have done that. But anyway, what happened next?'

'Then they talk me about the job. Say what I be doing. And the college. They tell me furry much information about the work, I write it all down so no forget. Then they tell me wait outside in a different room, but I hear them talking.'

'What did they say?'

'They say they wanting three persons. The big man he got loud voice, he say that now they got all three, and the others say him yes. Then they tell me come back in, so I going.'

'Did they offer you the job?'

'Not yet. Is many steps yet. The big man he gone, but the nice lady still there with the fat lady. They make fill in the forms and I got the student visa application. They say they call me tomorrow and if is good can I go the England next month visit the college. I say yays, of course. I say I furry like go the England and that's it. Go home then.'

'Oh, Pedro, I do hope they say yes. You will ring me tomorrow as soon as you know, won't you?'

-ooOOoo-

'Its 2 Easton Drive, Geoff. I feel so silly, but …'

'What about 2 Easton Drive, love? What's the matter?'

'I'm so sorry, Geoff. I know you will hate me after we made such plans, but I've lived here all my life and … and … and finding that little house suddenly made it all very real to me.'

Geoff passed Janet another tissue and forced himself to let her take her time.

'Take your time, love,' he said. 'What's the problem.'

'Oh, Geoff! I don't want to leave 2 Easton Drive. I'm so sorry … it's stupid I know but there are so many memories here … I love you so much and I would do anything for you, but please don't make me sell 2 Easton Drive …'

Janet buried her face in her hands and sobbed.

'What?' said Geoff, 'You mean you don't want to sell the house? You want to stay here?'

'Oh, Geoff ….'

'Well, that's wonderful news!'

'I'm so sorry …'

'No, I'm serious. I've always loved this house and I have wanted to live round here for years!'

'Really? Geoff, you are not just saying this,' hiccuped Janet.

'No, I'm deadly serious! I only went along with buying a different house because I thought it is what you wanted. I would love to stay living here!'

'Honestly?'

'If you are here, I can think of nothing I would like more! And think of the money we will save!'

'But I thought …'

'Well, you thought wrong. I absolutely agree with staying here!'

'You're not cross with me?'

'Never!'

'And you really don't mind?'

Janet was smiling now.

'I really, really don't mind. In fact, I love the idea. And I love you too, Janet. Now please will you marry me?'

'Oops,' said Bobbie, turning on her heel at the bottom of the stairs and running back up again.

-ooOoo-

## Chapter 14

Mike joined five or six of his colleagues with their boss, in his office, for a hastily convened meeting.

'We have just heard from our counterparts in Spain,' he began. 'There will be an official statement later today, but they have told us that a major drugs ring from South America has been busted and with it a huge money-laundering business in Germany, the Netherlands and the UK has been exposed.'

Mike wondered where this was going and exchanged glances with his colleagues, who were obviously sharing his thoughts.

'This will affect us in various ways, some of which are not yet clear. But there is one immediate link to ongoing work in relation to that Spanish law firm and their London office. Mike, you will be interested to know that the German builder who invested in the law firm, who is now in custody in Spain, was receiving backing from a cartel of drug overlords to fund his operations. The Spanish are convinced that the money he invested in the law firm came from that source and think they can prove it.'

Mike shifted uncomfortably in his chair.

'I need hardly tell you that the pressure on us to prove that we throughly investigated the legitimacy of the Spanish law firm's funding lines will now become intense. We need to make sure all of our paperwork is squeaky-clean here. Mike, if you need to draw anyone in to help from other tasks, you can do so, and if Mike asks you, guys, please step up a.s.a.p as we must get this tidied up.'

-ooOoo-

'Yes, Rosy. He was absolutely proposing to her! I nearly walked in on them, but managed to back out and hide upstairs until the danger passed,' Bobbie twittered.

'Well, that is lovely. I liked your Uncle Geoff and Janet very much and wish them every happiness ..'

'But I think there might be a problem. I'm sure I heard Janet crying before that. I hope everything is OK. I had to leave for work before they were up so I haven't caught up with them yet.'

'Tears of joy, perhaps? Still, all will become clear when you get home, I'm sure. And hopefully your Uncle Geoff will also have some news about those three places for us to rent he is looking into.'

'Yes, that is exciting, isn't it. By the way, I'm going to get to meet Baldy Head, the M.D., this morning and I hope to get some tips from him on how to get new business. Then hopefully I can start to bring in some commission to take the pressure off the finances.'

-ooOoo-

Geoff could not stop smiling.

He called Ms. Susan Sanderson from Stiffhams Estate Agents and told her that they had changed their minds about the little house they viewed and wanted to withdraw their offer.

He delivered a letter from Janet to the estate agents telling them to take 2 Easton Drive off the market, apologise to the buyers, and explain that they were staying put.

Then, as he sat in his car, he called two agents and one rather shady-sounding character about the three properties to rent for Rosy and Bobbie, and made an appointment to see one of them when Bobbie came home from work.

And all through this he hummed a happy tune and felt that all was right with the world.

Janet had said yes, they were staying at 2 Easton Drive, Bobby was moving out and, because he did not now have to buy another house, he was about to become considerably better off. What a splendid place the world was, he thought.

But then, in the car park at the back of the estate agents, the old Jaguar refused to start.

-ooOOoo-

Orlando had found himself a job in a bar.

For a man of his qualifications it was a ludicrous thing to do, but he needed the money and applying for jobs with the lawyers in Madrid took time.

He had forgotten to shave for several days and was drinking rather more than was good for him. The scruffy little bar where he worked served rather lack-lustre tapas that he survived on, and the room he found in the damp and draughty boarding house opposite was convenient but nothing more, and he did not intend to stay there any longer than he needed to.

His father had stated that any and all communications had to be passed through the 'Human Resources Director' at the office and had effectively cut Orlando off.

He knew there was no point in trying to get in touch with Ingrid, she had made her position very clear in her last email, and he had begun to see that she was using him as much as he was using her.

He clung to the hope that his father had not 'blacklisted' him and that he would still be able to get a reference when, and if, he found a lawyer willing to offer him a job.

As the first customers shuffled into the squalid bar,

Orlando finished his coffee and got ready to work.

-ooOoo-

## Chapter 15

'And as you see there is plenty of space at the side to widen it up and extend it to make a double garage, so both our cars can be under cover.' Geoff was making plans for 2 Easton Drive.

'They have done something very similar round the corner,' Janet said, 'but they extended over the top as well and added a granny-flat.'

'Well, obviously we don't need a granny-flat, love,' Geoff replied, thinking fleetingly that if such accommodation was provided they would never winkle Bobbie out of it, 'but it does indicate that there ought not to be any problem with the Local Council over planning permission.'

'Fair enough, Geoff, if you want to do it, then go ahead and get some builders in for quotes.'

'And just to be clear, I am paying for all this. No argument. We can also go and choose the new kitchen on Saturday if you like.' Geoff was pleased to be doing something positive, and now that they were definitely staying at 2 Easton Drive, he wanted to show Janet that he was committed to making their home as pleasant as possible.

As they turned to walk back inside, Geoff was delighted to see his Jaguar coming down the road having been repaired, with Gary the mechanic grinning widely at the wheel.

Soon the old car would be cosseted in a garage of its own, snuggled up next to Janet's car, and although they had not decided on dates yet, in the not to distant future Janet and Geoff would be married, and all of life for Geoff seemed absolutely perfect.

-ooo0oo-

The flat was over the top of one of those increasingly rare old-fashioned ironmongers. The sort of place that sold those garden incinerators that look like dustbins with a chimney, and screws, singly or by the dozen. It was run by the third generation of a family dynasty that had operated the shop since shortly after it was built in the 1950s and, as a business, it was thriving.

The original owner had lived in the flat over the premises, but as time went on and the business became more successful, he bought himself a house and the flat was used as a first home by his children and then their children until they too moved on. Now, with no new generation on the horizon yet, it was surplus to requirements, and after a period being used as a store, had just been freshly refitted, decorated and carpeted ready to be let out.

It had two double bedrooms, a small boxroom and

a large lounge with a wide bay window at the front separated by a peninsular from the newly fitted open-plan kitchen. There was a cloakroom as well as a bathroom and stairs leading down to a private front door off a little courtyard set up with a narrow strip of grass and space to park a car behind a tall wooden gate.

Geoff, Janet and Bobbie were the first people to look at it and all three were very impressed.

'Now, we was going to let it furnished,' said Mr Winters, the ironmonger and current owner. 'And the rent we was asking assumes it would be furnished, like. Of course, if you wants to take it empty, I mean unfurnished, we can reduce that a bit, but on the other hand, if you agrees, we can let you know the furniture budget and you can pick your own furniture from the furniture store in East Woodham my cousin owns.'

Bobbie, who of course did not own a single stick of furniture thought that was a capital idea, and said so.

'He's got some nice stuff in there, Arthur has, and of course he is doing it at trade prices so you should find there is plenty in the budget to make it comfortable.'

'Well, this sounds marvellous,' said Geoff, 'and being almost opposite the station it is ideal for Rosy's commute to work. Do you think she will like it, Bobbie?'

Bobbie had been taking photographs and videos on her mobile phone and astonished Geoff when she said, 'Rosy says she likes it very much and will come over tomorrow for a look, but in the meantime, Mr Winters, if you would like us to put down a deposit now to secure it, either Rosy can organise a bank transfer or …'

'Or I could give you a cheque,' said Geoff, cottoning on quickly to the trend of the conversation.

'Thank you, Uncle Geoff,' said Bobbie. 'And we would like to take up the idea of choosing the furniture as you suggested, please. Perhaps, Janet, we could toddle over to East Woodham for a look on Saturday?'

Never one to turn down the opportunity to go shopping with Bobbie, Janet enthusiastically agreed and Geoff reached for his cheque book.

-ooOoo-

There were policemen everywhere.

The concierge was kept busy calling the lift or opening the door to the stairs and explaining where each department was and secretaries and receptionists were rushing about trying to deal with the influx of officialdom.

Orlando's father had left the building a couple of hours beforehand. His good relations with the Chief of Police over the years had paid off in the form of a tip-off as to what was about to happen.

He knew that the same thing was happening at the

same time in his offices in London, Alicante and Berlin and that negotiations on the joint venture they had been setting up with another lawyer in Rome had been abruptly bought to a halt by their Italian counterparts.

He packed his suitcases in the boot of the Bentley and headed off for the long drive to Marbella, where he maintained a large and very comfortable, but rarely visited estate with a private vineyard. The company that owned it was not listed as having any connection with him or his business and the directors were shadowy nominees who would be impossible to track down if anyone were to try.

The address was not recorded anywhere in his personal effects and as far as his business was concerned, it did not exist.

-oo0Ooo-

## Chapter 16

'I am confident,' the Minister was saying, 'that the very limited support given to this business was properly researched and that Her Majesty's Treasury and other departments put in place prudent measures and thorough-going, due diligence before becoming involved. There are very stringent rules on how Government operates when it promotes new investment into the UK and I can categorically state now that all protocols have been followed and continue to be followed in this matter.'

'Have there been any arrests yet?' called an intrepid press reporter to his disappearing back as the door of the Ministry closed behind him.

In South America, the Netherlands, Spain, Germany and France there had been many arrests, but in England, so far at least, nobody had been detained. The British police could find nobody to arrest, and the Spanish in Madrid only had the German builder and a handful of fairly low-level drug couriers in the cells. But in the Costa Blanca, and particularly Alicante, the pavements were being swept clean of the low life that traded in illegal drugs and the police were running out of space to put all those they arrested.

In Colombia and Mexico, where the most important arrests had been made, the information those captured were pouring out in an effort to save their own skins had resulted in the real drug bosses being identified and the routes they used to launder money were being disrupted.

In London, in an unconnected investigation, several large successful property development companies had been under investigation for months, or in some cases years, for selling blocks of property off to 'investors' who just left the flats and houses to rot and nobody ever moved in. Now, with the revelations from the squealing drug cartel bosses, the Metropolitan Police at last had the missing link and they moved in, in numbers, questioning the directors and chairmen of the development companies and gaining insight into the connections they had and who had bought all that property.

The odious, apparently entirely legal practice of selling property to shadowy companies was being unpicked at last.

-oo0Ooo-

Rosalind was not happy, but it had to be done.

Mike put in all sorts of extra hours and when, a week later, they could confirm to the Minister that their department had an absolutely scrupulous record as far as the paper trail was concerned, the external consultants turned their fire elsewhere.

Mike's boss came to see him. A rare occurrence in itself.

'Well done, Mike. That was excellent work. Thank you.' Mike made a deprecating gesture, but the boss had more to say. 'Now, how is that little baby of yours? Your wife must be quite bent out of shape having to cope on her own while you sweated away at this. Why don't you pull some holiday forward and take a week off to be with them. I'll sign it off for you.'

-oo0Ooo-

'Yays, so I coming the England in the … er … telf, I mean the twelve days time, stay the London in a hotel.' Pedro smiled into the FaceTime screen.

'What can't you stay with us? I'm sure Janet and Geoff won't mind,' said Bobbie.

'I sorry, is no allowed. All has to stay the same hotel and we only stay the two nights,'

'Well, why don't I come up to London to see you?'

'Oh, Bobbie, you no know how a much I love that, but is no allow. We a have go the dinner with the big bank blokes, they telling us all the things. We got the tour of the college early quick smart in the morning then the visit the big London bank then back the airport. Is no time for the looking. Just the work.'

'Oh dear. That is a pity. But isn't it exciting that you

have got through to the next stage! How do you feel about it?'

'I feeling furry frighten be honest. I hoping I good enough for this. My English she so poor maybe they no want me.'

'Your English, my adorable boy, is absolutely charming. I could listen to you for hours.'

'Yays, but you liking the Pedro, they not so sure.'

'Pedro. I don't just like you, you know.'

'Bobbie?'

'I more than like you.'

'Bobbie! You lovely. Dead certain, no question. You so pretty. I'm … how you say … abhor you little nose point in the air.'

'I hope you mean "adore"!'

'Yays, Yays! Adore, of course adore. Yays. You got amazing hair also and the eyes phenomenal.'

'Oh, Pedro. you are so sweet.'

'Bobbie … Bobbie. Now you get your flat … The Pedro, he come stay all the night with you?'

'No, Pedro. We have talked about this. I'm not like that. It's not that I don't fancy you … God knows I do … its just that … I want to wait.'

'Oh. I know. I remember you say. But the Pedro ….'

'I know, honey. Please be patient with me.'

'Yays. Yays. Of course Bobbie … I sorry, no mean upset.'

'Pedro.'

'Si?'

'Pedro, I have to go now. I love you Pedro. Goodnight.'

And she snapped her iPad shut and breathed a huge shuddering sigh. There, she had said it, but it wasn't easy being good.

-oo0Ooo-

The dinner party was not the sort of thing Geoff enjoyed, but Janet wanted to celebrate their engagement with friends and, checking up on his stock of indigestion tablets, he returned to the lounge where the guests were settling.

Lucy, Janet's friend from university, seemed to be cornered against the fireplace by Rosy Brice-Waterman who was recounting the tale of Bobbie and the swimming pool in between great bursts of laughter and much slapping of the thighs.

The elderly Sri-Lankan dentist and his equally elderly wife sat on a corner of the sofa and smiled their sixty-watt smiles at everyone, and Bobbie flitted about serving drinks.

'Where is Janet?' said Clive, accepting another scotch

from Bobbie.

'She is engaged in the kitchen, I think,' said Geoff.

'I thought she was engaged to you!' guffawed Clive.

It was going to be a long night.

-ooOOoo-

**Epilogue**

Rosy let out a satisfied sigh.

The email from Martina, the English-speaking lady at the Town Hall in the Costa Blanca, contained the Mayor's thanks for her help in starting an investigation which, as it turned out, had far reaching implications.

Had she not so painstakingly explained all that had gone on at Orlando's villa, they would not have sent in their own investigative team, and the fraud that certain Council Officials then uncovered would have remained buried.

As she would no doubt know by now, Martina's letter continued, her visit to the Town Hall opened up a huge investigation into international money laundering, for which the Mayor and the Council had been congratulated by the Government in Madrid.

On behalf of the Town Hall and the people of the little Spanish town it represented, the letter said, the Mayor wanted to give Miss Rosy Brice-Waterman his personal thanks and say that if she ever wanted to return to his corner of Spain they would make her most welcome and ensure that she was well entertained.

The letter finished with a fussy flowery signature from the Mayor himself which Martina had scanned from the original letter in Spanish.

The sound of clattering crockery in the kitchen paused for a minute.

'Bobbie,' she called. 'Have you ever heard that it is sometimes said that the flapping of a butterfly's wings in one part of the world can cause a hurricane on the other side of the globe. Well come and have a look at this.'
Bobbie came to look, 'I think we have made it clear to Orlando and his cronies that you don't mess with English girls, especially Girton Girls!'

'Blimey o'Reilly,' said Bobbie, 'When you mix it, they certainly stay mixed!'

'How are you getting on with setting up the kitchen?'

'It's done. Sort of,' giggled Bobbie. 'Shall we open another bottle of wine to celebrate our first night in our new home?'

'Another one?'

**The End ... for now.**

## Disclaimer:

Note: All rights reserved. No part of this book, ebook or manuscript or associated published or unpublished works may be copied, reproduced or transmitted by any means, electronic, mechanical, photocopying or otherwise, without the prior written permission of the author.
Copyright: Bob Able 2022

The author asserts the moral right under the Copyright, Design and Patents Act 1988 to be identified as the author of this work.

This is a work of fiction, Any similarities between any persons, living or dead and the characters in this book is purely co-incidental.
The author accepts no claims in relation to this work.

## Acknowledgements:

Thanks to Andy Crabb for all his help, guidance and painstaking proofreading and to my wonderful wife Bee, who puts up with me sitting up for hours on end writing this stuff and ignoring her.

With thanks to the works of P G Wodehouse. I decided to use the name Bassington as my personal tribute to that wonderful writer. His great creation, Jeeves, refers to the Bassington-Bassington family, from where I borrowed part of Bobbie's name. Written around 100 years ago, the great wit of Wodehouse is, in my opinion, still some of the funniest writing in the English language, and I'm sure Bobbie would agree!

Photo credit: Dominic Sansotta.

**Bob Able:**

If you like Bob Able's distinctive writing style and would like to read more of his work, here is a little more information…..

**About the author:**

**Bob Able** is a writer of fiction, thrillers and memoirs and describes himself as a 'part-time expat' splitting his time between coastal East Anglia in England, and the Costa Blanca in Spain.
He writes with a lighthearted touch and does not use graphic descriptions of sex or violence in his books, that is not his style. He prefers to leave that sort of thing to the reader's imagination.

**'Spain Tomorrow'**, the first book in his popular and amusing memoir series was the **third most popular travel book on Amazon** in late 2020 and with its sequel, **'More Spain Tomorrow'** it continues to attract many good reviews and an appreciative audience in Europe, the United Kingdom, the USA and beyond.

His fictional novels include **'Double Life Insurance'**, **'No Point Running'**, **'The Menace Of Blood'** (which is about inheritance, not gore) and the sequel **'No Legacy of Blood'** and are fast-paced engaging thrillers, with a touch of romance and still with that signature, gentle, Bob Able humour.

His semi-fictional memoir **'Silke The Cat, My Story'**, written with his friend and wine merchant, Graham Austin and Silke the Cat herself, is completely different. Cat lovers adore it and so do readers across the generations. Silke is a real cat, she lives today in the Costa Blanca, and her adventures which she recounts in this amusing book really happened.

All Bob's books are available from Amazon as paperbacks or ebooks.

**What's next?** Well, **'Double Life Insurance'** adds another thriller to the list where we first met Bobbie and several of the characters in 'Bobbie and the Spanish Chap' and there is a rumour of a third sequel to **'Spain Tomorrow'** in the pipeline.

What is more, <u>there is another 'Bobbie Bassington Story' coming!</u> **If you would like details please get in touch.**

<u>**'Bobbie and the Crime Fighting Auntie'**</u> **follows on from this book.**

**You can send Bob an email at the address below, to request details of release dates.**

**The email address below is live and will reach him in person.**

**bobable693@gmail.com**

You can find details of how to buy all Bob's books and also follow him at:
**www.amazon.com/author/bobable**
Or just enter **Bob Able books** on the Amazon site and the full list should appear.

He also has a website, but hates updating it so don't expect too much!
**www.bobable693.wixsite.com/spain-tomorrow**

**Incidentally, Bob is looking for a new publisher and a 'literary agent' to represent him … any ideas?**